Exit 8

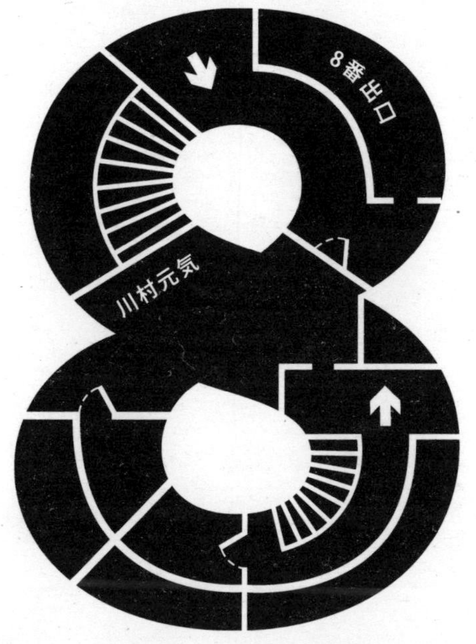

Exit 8

Exit 8

This novel is an adaptation of the film based on the original game by KOTAKE CREATE

Genki Kawamura

ITHAKA

First published in the UK in 2026 by Ithaka Press
An imprint of Bonnier Books UK
5th Floor, HYLO, 105 Bunhill Row, London, EC1Y 8LZ

Original game by KOTAKE CREATE
Original Japanese edition published by Suirinsha Ltd.
Original title: Hachiban deguchi
Copyright © Genki Kawamura, 2025
Translation rights reserved by Sameeha Anwar, 2026 under the license granted
by Genki Kawamura inc., Tokyo, arranged with Suirinsha Ltd., Tokyo.
All rights reserved.

This is a work of fiction. Names, places, events and incidents are either the
products of the author's imagination or used fictitiously. Any resemblance to
actual persons, living or dead, or actual events is purely coincidental.

A CIP catalogue record for this book is available from the British Library.

Hardback ISBN: 978-1-80617-390-7
Paperback ISBN: 978-1-80617-391-4

Also available as an ebook and an audiobook

1 3 5 7 9 10 8 6 4 2

Original book cover designed by KENJIRO SANO (MR_DESIGN INC.)
UK book cover designed by Jake Cook, Bonnier Books Art Dept.
Images by Toho Co., Ltd
Map and information poster adapted by Envy Design Ltd
Design and Typeset by IDSUK (Data Connection) Ltd
Printed and bound by CPI(UK) LTD, Croydon, CR0 4YY

The authorised representative in the EEA is Bonnier Books UK (Ireland) Limited.
Registered office address: Block B, The Crescent Building,
Northwood, Santry, Dublin 9, D09 6X8, Ireland
compliance@bonnierbooks.ie
www.bonnierbooks.co.uk

Abandon all hope, ye who enter here.
Dante Alighieri, *The Divine Comedy*

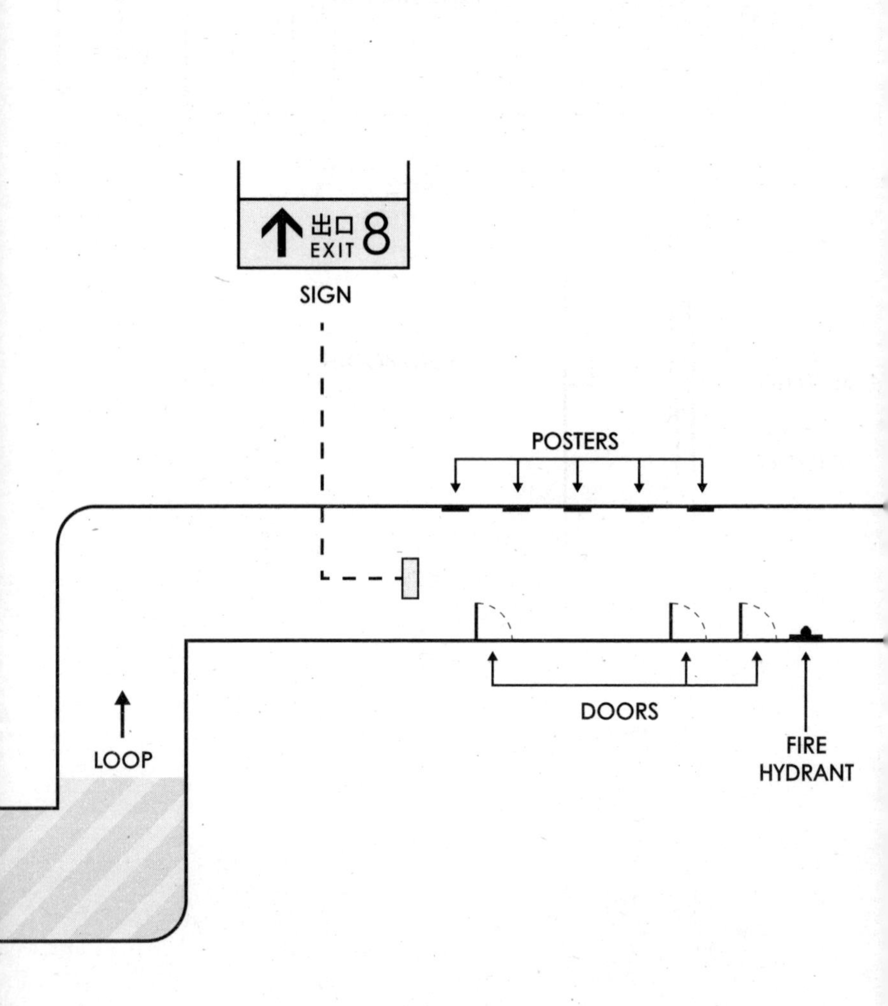

出口
EXIT 8
SIGN
POSTERS
DOORS
LOOP
FIRE
HYDRANT

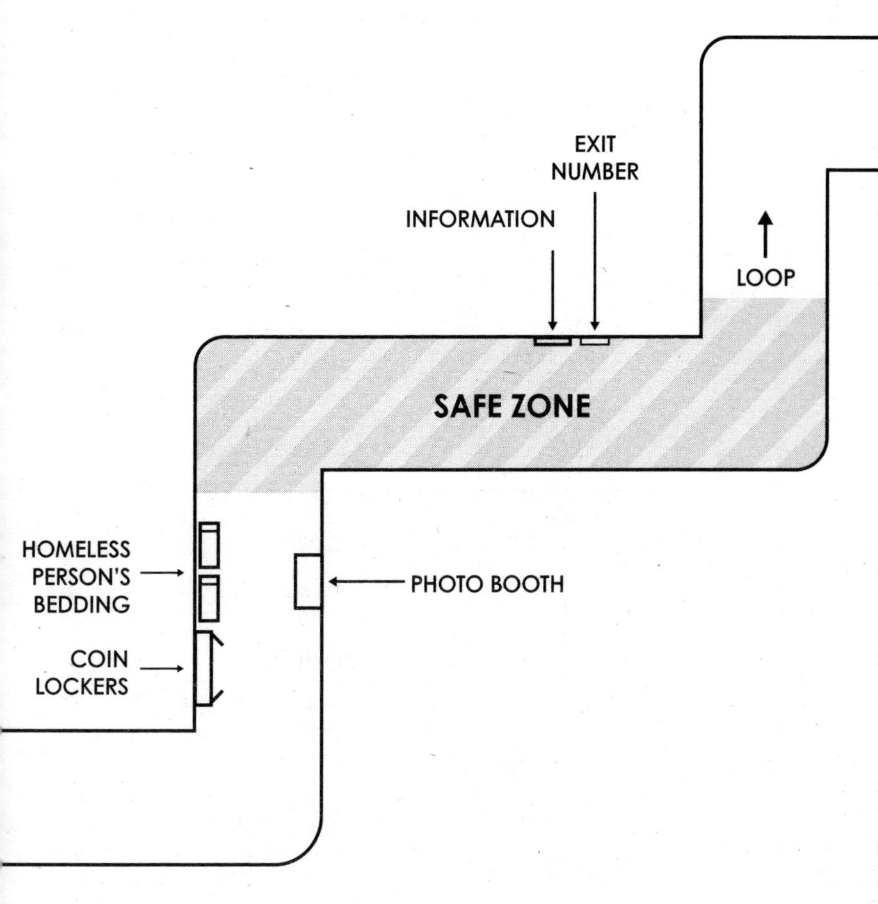

INFORMATION
EXIT
NUMBER
LOOP
SAFE ZONE
HOMELESS
PERSON'S
BEDDING
COIN
LOCKERS
PHOTO BOOTH

(ご案内　Information)

異変を見逃さないこと
Do not overlook any anomalies.

映画を先に楽しみたければ、すぐに引き返すこと
If you would like to experience the film first,
turn back immediately.

小説を先に楽しみたければ、引き返さないこと
If you would like to experience the novel first,
do not turn back.

小説で明かされる秘密を、決して他人には言わないこと
Do not reveal the secrets unveiled in the novel.

8番出口から外に出ること
Go out through Exit 8.

0 THE SUBWAY

It sounded like the wail of a newborn.

I took off my earphones and shifted my gaze towards the sound. A woman was sitting in the priority seats holding a crying baby in her arms. The subway car was packed. Commuters clung to straps and handrails, their eyes glued to their screens as if they couldn't hear the baby's cries.

'We're almost at the hospital, just a little longer,' the mother whispered to her child. It must have a fever. Red in the face, the baby continued to cry despite its mother's attempts to soothe him. She seemed acutely aware of the people around her, reacting to every sigh and cough as though they were unspoken complaints. Someone gasped for breath, taken over by a fit of coughs. Then, like floodgates bursting, a voice exploded through the air.

'Shut that thing up!'

My shoulders jumped. I timidly turned my head to see who had shouted. A man in a suit stood across from the mother and baby. He was probably on his way to work. He ran a hand through his unkempt hair and trembled in his rumpled suit, his voice growing more heated. 'Everyone's sick of it! You're the mother – make it stop!'

'I'm sorry. . .' The woman hunched over her child and bowed her head repeatedly. Startled by the shouting, the baby let out an even louder scream.

'What kind of person drags a baby onto a packed train? Have some damn sense. You're torturing the kid too!'

At that moment, the train jolted as the brakes kicked in. The man stumbled, crashing into another passenger before slamming his head against the door between cars. 'Goddammit!'

His voice crackled with rage.

Clutching a strap for support, he leaned forwards until his face was close to the baby's.

The mother glared up at him. His greasy hair stuck to his forehead, which was furrowed deep with anger. 'You got some nerve looking at me like that. You think I'm the bad guy here, huh? I'm just saying what everyone else is thinking!'

He gestured wildly, trying to draw agreement from the people around him, but no one responded. The passengers stayed glued to their phones, silent and motionless. His murky eyes drifted in my direction, and I quickly turned away to face the front.

In the train window, I caught a glimpse of myself – white earphones dangling from my hand, pale skin, cracked lips and dark circles beneath bloodshot eyes. I felt repulsed by the man and helpless at my own inaction. But instead of confronting either, I slipped the earphones back in, as if sealing it all off. I tapped one lightly. *Pop.* The noise-cancelling kicked in, and all the sound around me vanished.

Turning my gaze from the real and uncomfortable, I looked down at my phone and opened my X app. A first-person shooter appeared on the screen – someone firing a machine gun inside a ruined building. Ear-splitting explosions. Spurts of blood. The screen wavered and blurred, and the words 'GAME OVER' floated into view. An ad for a new war game.

I scrolled my feed, and a boy screaming in the rubble filled my screen. It was probably somewhere in the Middle East, after a bombing. Dark blood ran down his face as he wandered through the remains of a city. I scrolled again. Footage of a city being bombed under a night sky. I could no longer tell whether these images were real or just part of a game.

As I scrolled, the fiery explosion unfolding across the night sky gave way to high-school girls in uniform, dancing to a pop hit. I scrolled down further to see a cat hopping around on two legs.

A model posing with a luxury handbag. Two men brawling inside a convenience store. A lab rat with a human ear growing from its back. Teenagers attacking a homeless man in an underpass. A president somewhere delivering a provocative speech. An influencer offering a detailed rundown of cosmetic surgery procedures.

With every flick of my thumb, all kinds of images spilled out in a never-ending stream, appearing and disappearing in an instant. It all seemed random, but apparently this was content selected by AI, based on my viewing and search history. If that's true, then maybe this endless feed of images is just a mirror of my soul.

Turning away from the crying baby and the shouting man, and turning a blind eye to the tragedies on my feed – somehow they felt like the same thing.

I swiped my thumb across the screen. A butterfly flitted through a luxury resort in one clip, followed by a job ad for temporary staff. Then, the low rumble of a siren, like the sound of the earth groaning, poured through my headphones. I stopped moving my thumb and stared at the screen. A coastal town was being swallowed by a tsunami. Houses, boats, everything reduced to rubble in an instant. A boy was screaming, fleeing from the surging wave. I tensed, my body rigid, as I watched the muddy waters engulf the town. Then a soft chime sounded through my earphones, and a message popped up: *Where are you?*

I opened my messaging app. The sender's icon was a black cat – it was from my ex. We had broken up just last month, after being together for years. There hadn't been a clear reason or cause. But a certain incident had cast a lingering shadow on our relationship – a shadow that only grew darker with time, until we could no longer see how we felt about each other. We broke up, as if to escape it. There was sadness, of course, but also a strange sense of relief. I think she must've felt it too. So then, why was she texting me now? Puzzled, I moved my thumb and typed out a response.

I'm on the subway. About to arrive at today's temp job. What's up?

I'm at the doctor's.

What's wrong?

I'm pregnant.

My finger froze above the screen. I stared at the message, unable to reply. Another one followed.

I can't believe this happened right after we decided to break up.

A baby's cry echoed in my ears. I couldn't tell if it was coming from inside the train, or from the hospital on the other end of the line.

What do we do? Her messages kept arriving, each one punctuated by that soft chime. I felt my chest tighten. I looked up from my screen and saw my own distressed face reflected in the train window. Light streaking past. A baby crying. A man shouting. Straps swaying overhead. I felt like I had seen this scene before, somewhere.

What do we do? I asked myself, just as the train pulled into my stop. I pushed through the crowd towards the doors, catching a glimpse of the infant. Still wailing. The mother, bowing again and again in apology. The man, still yelling. Around them, commuters stood motionless, blank-faced, eyes glued to their phones. The whole scene looked surreal, like a pantomime on a stage.

Swept along by the tide of people, I stepped onto the platform and began climbing the stairs with unsteady feet. From beyond my earphones, I could faintly hear the melody that signalled the next train's arrival. I recognised it – Maurice Ravel's *Boléro*. My mother used to love that piece when I was a child. A single melody repeated over and over, gradually rising as if it were spiralling upwards. Even the rumble of the subway sounded like its rhythm now. Moving in step with that rhythm, I became part of the neatly ordered grey column ascending the stairs. I glanced down at my phone again, still unsure what to say. Then, it rang.

'Hello?' I answered, my earphones still in.

Silence. Faintly, I could hear a baby fussing on the other end of the line. My ex was probably in the waiting room at the OB/GYN.

'Hello?' I asked again.

A raspy voice finally responded. 'You saw my messages?'

'I did.'

'What do we do about the baby?'

I stopped halfway up the stairs, completely at a loss. The soft whimpering in the background turned into full-on crying.

'Move it!' barked a large man behind me, jolting me back to reality.

'Sorry . . .' I mumbled, bowing my head. He shot me a glare as he brushed past. I averted my gaze and started climbing again.

'I guess you still can't decide,' she said, her voice tinged with resignation.

'Huh?'

'You always said you couldn't picture yourself as a parent . . .'

I couldn't find the words. I just kept walking. I reached the top of the stairs and headed towards the ticket gates.

'I felt the same way too, about starting a family. I just couldn't do—'

Her voice cut off suddenly. A man in a rush slammed into my shoulder, and my phone slipped from my hand, clattering to the floor. I yanked out my earphones and picked it up. Ticket gate chimes, a cascade of footsteps, the low rumble of the subway flooded into my ears all at once. Pain throbbed in my shoulder where he'd hit me. I looked down at my phone. The upper-left corner of the screen was shattered, a deep crack running through it. I'd only bought it three months ago. Sighing, I put my earphones back in. Her voice returned.

'. . . and when the doctor said that, I started thinking about it more seriously. She was right – it's not something I can deal with on my own. That's why I called you.' I strained to piece together what I'd missed. Then she asked, 'Are you even listening?'

'Hm? Uh-huh.' I gave a vague reply as I tapped my phone at the ticket gate and stepped through. I turned right and began climbing a narrow, dim stairwell. Back when we were together, she used to ask me that all the time – *Are you listening?* To her, it seemed like I was always distracted, always missing the things that mattered.

'What do we do?' I could hear babies crying on her end of the phone. A tight knot of panic and guilt clenched in my chest. I started coughing.

'Which hospital are you at? I'll ask if I can get the day off.' Still coughing, I slipped off my grey nylon backpack, unzipped it and started digging around inside. After sifting through a bottle of water, a power bank, a small towel and extra masks, I finally found my asthma inhaler. I put it to my lips and inhaled deeply.

'You don't have to go out of your way. . .' she said, in a pitying voice.

'No, it's fine. Really.'

I took a deep breath to steady myself and started up the dark stairwell towards the exit.

'I've already made up my mind,' she said.

'You've . . . made up your mind?'

When I didn't know what to say, I just echoed her words – something she used to call me out on all the time when we were together.

'I've decided what I'm going to do.'

'Wait,' I said, flustered, coughing as I broke into a run. 'I'm coming. I'll be there soon.'

'I . . . keeping . . .' Her voice was breaking up.

'Hello? The signal might be bad.'

'. . . not keeping it.'

'Hello?'

'Not-not-not . . . keeping-keeping-it-it-it-it-it-it.'

Her voice fell into a bizarre, mechanical loop, rising to a shrill pitch before cutting out altogether.

'Hello? Hello??'

I reached the top of the stairs and glanced at my phone. No signal. The antenna icon was gone.

'What the hell . . .'

Then I noticed the time on the cracked screen: 88:88. Had the fall broken it? Why now, of all times? I jabbed at the screen in frustration, but the call wouldn't go through. 'Damn it,' I muttered, taking out my earphones. I glanced sideways at a middle-aged man passing by as I rushed forwards.

Ahead, a long passageway stretched out before me. The walls were lined with white square tiles that reflected the cold glow of fluorescent lights. A yellow panel hung from the ceiling, emblazoned with the words '↑ Exit 8' in bold black letters.

On the left wall, there were six posters: an ad for a dental clinic, a promo for an M.C. Escher exhibition at a museum, a notice from a judicial scrivener's office. These were placed next to a flyer for a beauty clinic, a recruitment ad for high-paying part-time work and a subway manners poster. To the right, a sign with a large eye icon indicated that security cameras were in operation. There were three metal doors lined up on the wall on the right, with a fire hydrant next to them. Each door was labelled: Electrical Room, Employees Only and Terminal Test Valve Room. Two exhaust vents loomed above.

Still keeping an eye on the reception icon on my phone, I turned left at the end of the corridor. A row of coin lockers lined the wall – seventeen of them in all. At the far end sat a photo booth.

I caught a glimpse of my distressed face in the narrow mirror fixed to the front of the photo booth. Between the coin lockers and the booth, I noticed a blue tarp and pieces of cardboard laid out across the floor. On top of them, dirty blankets and grimy bags were heaped into a small mound. Scattered in front were paper cups from familiar coffee and fast-food chains, a few of them holding coins. It looked like a homeless person's sleeping spot, but no one was there.

I turned right again, and a tall yellow sign with an arrow came into view. It pointed towards Exit 0.

'Zero?' I murmured in puzzlement. The number felt off. Beneath it were names of places I didn't recognise: Nanbu Park, Mizuse Junior High School, Yonago Temple, Narihara Building, Happongi Crossing. It made no sense – how could all these places be ones I'd never even heard of?

My phone still read 'no service'. I had to get outside. I had to get to the hospital. I picked up my pace, turned left, then right – then left and right again – only to find myself pausing once more in confusion. In front of me stretched the same white underground passage. On the ceiling, a yellow sign reading ↑ Exit 8. Six posters on the wall. The security camera sign. Three metal doors. A fire hydrant. Two exhaust vents above.

I was sure I'd just seen this.

I felt bewildered but kept walking. Under the ↑ Exit 8 sign, I passed a middle-aged man. He looked like the typical salaryman: thinning hair, scruffy beard, white shirt, black slacks, leather shoes. He had a briefcase in his right hand, a smartphone in his left.

Proceeding warily, I turned left at the end of the corridor. There were the coin lockers. The photo booth. The homeless person's bedding between them. Another turn – and again, the yellow Exit 0 sign. The exact same scenery. I pushed forwards, took another left, then right, then left and right again, and stopped dead in my tracks. My eyes widened.

'What the . . .?'

Stretching out before me, once again, was a long, white underground passageway. And glowing above, in bold letters: ↑ Exit 8. Six posters on the wall. The security camera sign. Three metal doors. A fire hydrant. Two exhaust vents above.

'How is this possible . . .?'

A middle-aged man approached from ahead. He looked exactly like the one I had passed earlier. Briefcase in his right hand, smartphone in his left. He walked with the precise rhythm of a metronome, his leather shoes clicking on the floor. His eyes stayed fixed straight ahead – he didn't so much as glance at me as he passed.

I hurried down the passage and turned left at the corner. There they were again: the coin lockers, the photo booth, the bedding tucked into the gap between them. The narrow mirror on the side of the booth reflected my face back at me. My mouth was slightly open, my eyes wild. The sight sent a jolt of unease through me.

I strode quickly to shake off the feeling and rounded the corner. The sign for Exit 0 appeared again. It was filled with the same names I didn't recognise: Nanbu Park, Mizuse Junior High School, Yonago Temple, Narihara Building, Happongi Crossing. Something was very wrong. I quickened my pace, turned left, then right, then left and right again – then stopped cold. A long white underground passageway stretched out before me. On the ceiling was a sign that read ↑ Exit 8.

'It's the same passage . . .'

I was walking through the same place over and over again. The click of leather shoes echoed from up ahead. I looked up and stiffened. The thinning hair. The stubbled chin. White dress shirt, black slacks. Briefcase in one hand, smartphone in the other.

'It's the same guy . . .' I blurted, trembling. He walked forwards in a steady rhythm, his gaze fixed straight ahead. I watched him go out of the corner of my eye. Then, the sound of footsteps stopped.

Why did he stop? Heart pounding, I slowly turned round. He was smiling. But it wasn't a normal smile. It looked like a rubber mask had been stretched over his face.

A sharp gasp slipped from my throat as I backed away. The man stood frozen in place, the same fixed grin on his face. He didn't blink. Didn't twitch. It was like time had stopped around him. I couldn't tell if the expression meant joy or rage – it was impossible to read.

Keeping one eye on him, I edged down the passageway, rounded the next corner – and ran. The lockers, the bedding, the photo booth flashed past in my peripheral vision. And again, the sign appeared: Exit 0. Zero. Again.

My breath caught in my throat, panic rising. A ragged cough burst from my chest. Gasping for air, I turned back. He wasn't there. Relieved, I fumbled in my backpack, pulled out my inhaler and took a long breath from it. After a few deep breaths to calm myself, I moved forwards and turned the corner.

The long white corridor stretched before me once more. The sign pointing to Exit 8 hung from the ceiling. The man, whose face was plastered with a grin earlier, was walking towards me with his usual blank expression.

'This isn't the way out.'

I spun on my heel and hurried back the way I'd come. I didn't want to be anywhere near that man again. I ran round the corner – but what I saw made me gasp.

I was retracing my steps. The Exit 0 sign should have been on my right. But there it was – on my left. Had the space warped? Or was my mind playing tricks on me? I turned another corner and froze in place again.

'How is this possible?!'

Before me, the same long white passage. The same ↑ Exit 8 sign. Even when I turned round, the same corridor stretched behind me. The same man came walking towards me again. Steady pace. Unwavering stare. Not even a glance in my direction.

My pulse was pounding now, beating so hard it throbbed in my ears. The man kept walking, rounded the corner and disappeared.

If I stayed here any longer, I was going to lose my mind. I had to get help. I spotted the security camera on the ceiling and began waving my arms frantically.

'Hey!!'

The black lens inside the dome faced me, but I didn't feel like I was being seen. I turned to the fire hydrant and slammed the emergency button. It gave a dry, useless click.

I tried the doorknobs of the heavy metal doors, one after the other – Electrical Room, Employees Only, Terminal Test Valve Room. All of them were locked.

There was no way out. Hopelessness hit me like a wave. I slumped back against the cold concrete wall and stared blankly at the poster across the corridor. It was for an M.C. Escher exhibition.

Maurits Cornelis Escher – a twentieth-century Dutch artist known for his impossible architectures and endless staircases. He used a technique called *trompe l'oeil* to create optical illusions. Back in school, I'd never been particularly interested in art. But for a while, I'd been obsessed with Escher's drawings. I wasn't athletic and I didn't care much for classical literature, but maths had always come easily to me, and I was fascinated by architecture. Maybe that's why Escher's work, with its mathematical quality, had spoken to me the way it did.

The poster before me featured one of his illusions: nine ants crawling endlessly along a Möbius strip – a twisted surface with only one side, looping in on itself like the ∞ symbol. A path with no beginning, no end.

I stepped closer and stared at it. The Möbius strip curled like the figure 8. The ants were locked in eternal motion, forever circling the same track. I realised I was in the same situation. Desperate for any clue that might lead to an exit, I reached out and traced the line of ants with my finger.

A sharp, metallic smell like rust hit my nose. I looked up. A line of dark, red-black blood was trickling down the wall, creeping over the poster. I staggered back and tilted my head towards the ceiling.

A pool of blood had gathered there.

From above came muffled, distant noises – something like an explosion, followed by the layered groans and shrieks of people in pain. The pool spread rapidly across the ceiling, pulsing in sync with the rising cries. Then, it spilled down, dripping onto the the ↑ Exit 8 sign directly above me.

I felt a warm sensation on my cheek and touched it with my fingertips. Thick, sticky blood.

'Shit!'

As I scrubbed my fingers together, the pungent stench of blood stung my nose. I wiped my hand on my sleeve and turned back the way I'd come, retracing my steps. I rounded a corner, and there he was again – the salary-man. He was staring intently at his phone, not moving a muscle. I passed him as he stood motionless with his smartphone in his hand, like a wax figure. I approached the sign ahead, and then I saw it.

Exit 1.

I let out an involuntary 'Huh?'

The number had changed. It had been zero before, but now it was one. Why? Did it have something to do with the blood? Searching for answers, I stepped closer. Next to it was a sign I hadn't paid attention to before.

'Information . . .?'

I must have missed it because it was so inconspicuous. I took a closer look. It wasn't your usual information board.

I leaned in and read aloud: 'Do not overlook any anomalies . . . If you find an anomaly, turn back imme-diately . . . If you do not find any anomalies, do not turn back . . . Go out through Exit 8.'

Who had put this up, and why? It couldn't have been the subway staff. Was it some kind of prank? But if so, it was disturbingly elaborate. Staring at the sign, a thought crept in: What if this deranged place was some kind of computer program?

The blood – was that an 'anomaly'? And because I turned back after encountering it, the number advanced from zero to one? Then, what about the salaryman earlier? Was *his smile* an anomaly? Realising there were 'rules' behind all these absurd phenomena gave me a faint glimmer of hope.

Find the anomalies.

If I find one – turn back.

If I don't find one – move forwards.

If I kept repeating these steps, then maybe, just maybe, the numbers would continue to climb, from one to two, two to three . . . and eventually, I'd reach Exit 8. And get out.

I didn't know how much faith I could place in that strange sign. But right now, it was all I had. I had to believe. I had to get out of here and get to *her*.

'Do not overlook any anomalies . . . If you find an anomaly, turn back immediately . . . If you do not find any anomalies, do not turn back . . . Go out through Exit 8.' I repeated the words under my breath like a mantra. Then, I quickly turned the corner. The passage ahead was the same as ever – long, white, sterile. The glow of the ↑ Exit 8 sign. It hung from the ceiling with the silent authority of a god.

出口
Exit 8

1 THE LOST MAN

I hurried towards the Escher poster. The blood was gone.

'What? Where did it go?'

The long white underground passageway stretched out before me. Hanging from the ceiling was the ↑ Exit 8 sign. Everything was spotless – the ceiling, the floor, the walls. Not a trace of blood. I turned my palms upwards. No blood. Not even that rusty stench. The passage was enveloped in silence, as if nothing had ever happened.

So it *had* been an anomaly. The sign might really be telling the truth.

'I have to look out for anomalies . . .' I muttered to myself. Just then, I heard footsteps approaching. The man in the suit was walking towards me from the far end of the passageway.

'Hey! Excuse me!' I called out, running up to him. His movements seemed to be pre-programmed, running on repeat. He'd walk down the passage, no expression on his face, turn left at the end, then turn right at the next corner and then stop to look at his phone. Was that smile from earlier a glitch in his programming? But what if he was just following the same rules I was? Maybe he'd seen the information board too.

'You're lost, aren't you? I'm stuck here too.'

No response. He kept walking straight ahead, expressionless, eyes fixed forwards.

'Do you know where Exit 8 is? Maybe we could work together, look for anomal—' I stepped directly into his path, trying to stop him. But it was like I wasn't even there. His blank gaze never wavered, and I had to step aside to avoid a collision. He walked right past me, turned the corner and disappeared.

Talking with him seemed impossible. I was on my own.

'Anomalies . . . anomalies . . .'

I turned back towards the corridor, scanning every detail as I walked. Anomalies were bugs in the system. That's what this was. And finding bugs was what I did – I was a programmer, after all.

'No anomalies.' I murmured the words, then turned the corner. Lined up against the wall were the coin lockers, the photo booth and the makeshift bed wedged between them. At first glance, there was nothing unusual, no blood pools like earlier. The scene looked exactly the same as before. Good. No anomalies. I pressed ahead and turned right, expecting to find the sign for Exit 2.

But what I saw made me freeze.

Exit 0.

I stared in disbelief. Where had I gone wrong? What had I missed? I traced the words on the information board with my fingertips and read them aloud again.

'Do not overlook any anomalies . . . If you find an anomaly, turn back immediately . . . If you do not find any anomalies, do not turn back . . . Go out through Exit 8.'

I didn't spot any anomalies, so I had moved forwards. I must have missed something.

'Anomalies . . . anomalies . . .' I repeated the words under my breath like a mantra as I rounded the corner. There it was, the same long, white passage. The same ↑ Exit 8 sign hung from the ceiling.

I checked the posters on the left wall: 'Dental Clinic . . . Escher Exhibit . . . Judicial Services . . .' Had the images changed? The text? The font? 'Beauty Clinic . . . High-Paying Part-time Jobs . . . Subway Manners . . .'

But my memory was hazy. Unreliable. Everything was starting to look suspicious. After checking the posters, I stopped in front of the security camera sign. The symbol on it – a pair of large, stylised eyeballs – seemed to stare directly at me. I stared back. A bead of sweat trickled down from my temple, slid along my jawline and dropped to the floor.

I pulled my phone from my pocket and opened the camera app. One by one, I photographed each poster. *Click. Click. Click.* The sound of the shutter echoed through the passageway.

If I had photographic evidence, I could confirm whether there were any anomalies. I didn't know yet if this round was anomaly-free, but at least I'd have a record to check against. Just then, I heard footsteps behind me and glanced up.

'The salaryman again.'

I hurried towards him, jumped in front of his path and pointed the camera at him. I tapped the shutter. Not even a twitch. Even with a phone in his face, he walked on, expressionless. I watched him disappear down the corridor, then turned my attention to the wall on the right. I photographed the fire hydrant, the doors, the exhaust vents.

'Fire hydrant . . . door . . . door . . . exhaust vent . . . door . . . exhaust vent.'

No anomalies in sight. I checked my phone to make sure the photos were saved, then turned the corner at the end of the hallway.

'Lockers . . . blanket . . . photo booth,' I murmured the checklist aloud, photographing each item in turn. When I was done, I glanced back down the hallway to double-check. Still nothing out of place.

'No anomalies.'

I confirmed aloud, pointing forwards for good measure. Then I faced ahead and turned the final corner.

Exit 1.

'All right!'

The number had changed. I pumped my fist in relief. This was the first time I'd been able to answer correctly myself – no anomalies. I'd documented everything I needed to check with photos.

'All right. I've got this now.' I rounded the corner with confidence.

The white passageway stretched out before me. I looked at the ↑ Exit 8 sign before looking down at my phone.

'What . . .?'

The photo I'd just taken was blank, washed in a solid yellow.

'How . . .?'

I scrolled frantically through my photo gallery. Every photo I had taken in the passage was the same: a blank yellow screen, as if they'd been smeared in yellow paint. They were useless.

'Dammit!'

Desperate, I opened my messaging app.

My ex's message appeared on the screen, the one I hadn't been able to respond to. *What do we do?* The icon at the top of the screen read, 'No Service'.

Either way, I had to get out of here. I steadied my breathing, looked ahead and pointed up at the sign hanging from the ceiling.

'Exit 8 . . .'

Turning left, I began to check the posters again.

'Dental Clinic . . . Escher Exhibit . . . Judicial Services . . . Beauty Clinic . . . High-Paying Part-time—'

The footsteps of the salaryman passing by stopped.

I slowly turned my head in unease. He had stopped exactly where he had stopped before, wearing the exact same grin. He was standing perfectly still, facing my way with his rubber-mask smile.

'If you find an anomaly . . . turn back immediately . . .' I whispered to myself, trying to stay calm. Avoiding the man, I began to make my way back. But he followed. His head rotated towards me with an eerie smoothness, as if driven by a motor. Too smooth. It didn't seem human.

And then, I felt it again – a presence at my back. I turned. He was right behind me. A strangled gasp escaped my throat. He was closer than ever. Still smiling. His face was so close, yet I couldn't hear a single breath. Trying to shake the horror off, I sped forwards.

But again, I felt him behind me. I turned once more. He was inches away now, that rubbery grin hovering just beyond the tip of my nose. My stomach knotted, a cough rose in my throat. But I couldn't let it out. I had a feeling that if I made a sound, something terrible would happen.

It felt like a game of Red Light, Green Light. But if he caught me, what would he do to me?

I stared into the black voids of his eyes, took two steps back, then three, and then I turned and ran. Even as I sprinted, I could sense him gaining on me. I turned and saw him barrelling down the corridor at full speed, that same frozen smile on his face, his chest puffed out, arms swinging in exaggerated strides.

I stumbled as I turned the corner in panic and fell hard. He was right behind me now – I could feel it. My body seized in a coughing fit.

'Somebody . . . help . . .' My voice was cracked, a feeble mix of coughs and moans. When I looked up, there he was – staring intently into his phone. He was holding it in his usual pose. He wasn't panting. He hadn't broken a sweat. The man stood frozen, as if time itself had stopped around him.

I held my breath and approached the signboard.

Exit 2.

Relief washed over me, followed by another round of violent coughing. Gasping, I unzipped my backpack, pulled out my inhaler and took a deep breath. Then, I collapsed onto the floor beneath the sign.

In the corridor, the salaryman stood motionless, staring at his phone. Why was he here? Why had he chased me like that? Is it just the two of us trapped in this underground maze? If I couldn't find the anomalies, if I couldn't reach Exit 8, would I eventually become like him?

Fear surged through my chest. I gulped down the water from the plastic bottle in my bag. I exhaled and wiped my mouth on my sleeve. 'Exit 3 . . . here I come.' I forced the words out, trying to psych myself up, and turned the next corner.

The long white underground passage stretched out before me. Hanging from the ceiling was the ↑ Exit 8 sign.

'Dental Clinic . . . Escher Exhibit . . . Judicial Services . . . Beauty Clinic . . . High-Paying Part-time Jobs . . . Subway Manners.' I recited each poster aloud, scanning them one by one. Then – the sound of a camera shutter echoed from the end of the hall.

Printing your photo. A flat, robotic female voice followed.

Printing your photo. Printing your photo. Printing your photo. Printing your photo. Printing your photo. Printing your photo.

The same line repeated again and again, bouncing off the walls of the corridor. A loop.

An anomaly? Tensing up, I turned the corner.

Printing your photo.

The voice grew louder. It was coming from the photo booth. 'It's an anomaly.'

I approached the booth and froze.

The photo booth curtain had always been open, but this time it was drawn shut. Beneath it, I saw a pair of feet. There was someone here. But why were they taking a photo in a place like this?

'Um . . . excuse me . . .' My voice came out in a rasp.

No reply. Instead, *clack.* A photo slid out into the dispenser.

Your photo is ready, the robotic voice announced. The person inside hadn't moved at all.

I opened the dispenser and reached out for the photo.

I brought it up to my face, hesitantly. Eight identical ID photos, neatly aligned. Each one showed *me* – wearing the same rubbery smile as the salaryman.

'What . . .?' I whispered, letting the photo slip from my fingers.

From behind the curtain, I heard a cough. My body tensed as I moved my gaze to the sound. The shoes peeking out from under the booth shifted slightly – now pointing towards me, as if sensing my presence. The worn-out grey trainers looked familiar. I glanced down at my feet. The exact same trainers.

Could the person behind the curtain . . . be *me*? I felt compelled to pull the curtain back, to see who – or what – was in there. My fingers gripped the edge. But I couldn't do it. If I came face-to-face with whatever was in that booth, would I be able to hold on to my sanity?

Your photo is ready, The robotic voice cut through the silence.

Still frozen in place, my knees trembling, I watched another photo slide out of the machine. I looked at it. Me again – this time, with an even wider grin.

Your photo is ready. Your photo is ready. Your photo is ready. Your photo is ready. Your photo is ready. Your photo is ready.

With each announcement, the dispenser spat out photo after photo. Each one showed me smiling. With every new image, my smile grew unnaturally wider – mouth stretching too far, eyes widening into glossy, glass-like orbs, drained of life.

'This is an anomaly . . . it must be . . .'

I turned on my heel and hurried back the way I'd come.

Your photo is ready. Your photo is ready. Your photo is rea—

The announcement looped mechanically. When I turned the corner, the voice stopped.

Exit 3.

Seeing the number advance, I let out a big sigh of relief. A bead of sweat rolled down my temple. I put my hand to my face. My cheeks and forehead were soaked.

This space, with the numbered exit sign indicating whether I was correct or not, and the information board, might be a 'safe zone'. Every time I arrived, the anomalies would be 'reset' for the next round, it seemed.

One more piece of this strange underground puzzle had fallen into place. I turned the corner.

The long white underground passage. The ↑ Exit 8 sign hanging from the ceiling.

I went through the usual check: the posters, the salary-man, the doors and vents. Then I turned the corner. My eyes caught on the photo booth beside the lockers. This time, the curtain was open, and there was no one inside. The photos in the dispenser were all gone. Thinking back, that anomaly felt like a grim omen. I noticed my fingertips still trembled from when I'd touched the curtain.

This time, there didn't seem to be any anomalies.

Relieved, I started walking past the lockers. Then, I heard it. A baby, fussing. It was coming from behind me. I stopped and turned round. Soft breathing. Where was it coming from? I looked up and down the white passage. No one. Then the baby began crying, loud and clear. I kept my ears pricked as I retraced my steps. The crying seemed to be coming from inside the row of coin lockers.

'An anomaly . . .?'

I decided to turn back, but the crying grew louder. I spun round. What if this *isn't* an anomaly? Would I be walking away and letting a baby die?

What do we do? My ex's voice rang in my ears. I approached the locker in the centre row, where the crying was coming from. Slowly, I reached out and gripped the handle. As I pulled the door open just a crack, the crying grew louder from within.

'Hello?'

What was inside? The sound made my fingers tremble. My hand slipped off the handle and the door clicked shut. The crying came to a stop. Complete silence. I kept my eyes on the locker door. Not even the sound of breathing.

It had to be an anomaly.

Then, as I stepped back, all at once, cries erupted from *every* locker. Wailing. Screaming. The unmistakable shrieks of babies in distress. The metal doors shook violently as something from inside was pounding against them.

'Aagh!'

I stumbled, legs tangled, and crashed to the floor. Pain shot through my elbow as it hit the ground. I groaned.

'It's not my fault!' I curled up and covered my ears. The twisted cries filled the white passageway. The pounding on the locker doors grew fiercer, and the metal doors began to bulge outward, warped from the inside. The hinges were straining. Whatever was behind those doors, it was trying to get out.

'Stop . . . Stop . . . Please stop!!'

I staggered to my feet, glancing back, terrified that something might burst free. The crying chased me down the corridor.

Exit 4.

The second I saw the sign, the crying cut off. Silence returned. I doubled over coughing, gasping for air. It took a few deep breaths before my heart stopped racing. To steady myself, I rubbed my face with my palms, again and again. Then forced a smile.

'All right, halfway there.' I said it out loud, to keep myself together, and turned the corner.

There it was. The long white underground passage. The ↑ Exit 8 sign hanging from the ceiling.

'Dental Clinic . . . Escher Exhibit . . . Judicial Services . . . Beauty Clinic . . . High-Paying Part-time Jobs . . . Subway Manners . . . Salaryman.' I scanned the posters on the left-hand wall one by one.

'Security Cameras in Operation . . .?' After checking the line of posters and the walking man, I came to a stop in front of the sign. The massive cartoon eyeballs on the poster still seemed to be watching me. Unsettled, I turned my gaze back to the earlier posters. The bunny and bear on the Subway Manners poster. The anime girl in a maid outfit on the High-Paying Part-time Jobs ad. The beautiful young woman on the Beauty Clinic poster. Something about them felt . . . off.

But I couldn't double-check them with the photos I'd taken earlier – the photos were useless. Steeling myself, I turned to the other side of the passage and began inspecting the fire hydrant, metal doors and exhaust vents.

'Fire hydrant . . . door . . . door . . . vent . . .'

Suddenly, I felt something behind me. I spun round.

The cartoon eyes on the Security Camera sign looked like they were staring straight at me. Was I imagining it? I rubbed my eyes and looked again. No change. Just the same unblinking, forwards-facing gaze as before. I stepped closer and stared directly into the oversized eyes. Nothing. No movement. I must've been seeing things.

I paced back and forth in front of the posters five, six more times, checking and re-checking. The more I thought about it, the more uncertain I became. Was this an anomaly . . . or wasn't it? The deeper I sank into thought, the more *everything* started to seem like an anomaly. I'd made it all the way to Exit 4 – I couldn't let paranoia get the better of me and end up back at the start.

Right in front of me was the maid character from the Part-time Jobs poster. Something about her had changed. I stepped towards the poster, cautiously. She was looking straight at me. I felt eyes from the side too, and turned my head. The young women on the Beauty Clinic poster. The bunny and bear on Subway Manners. They'd all been looking straight ahead before, but now they were all staring at *me*.

'They're watching me . . .'

I had to risk it. I made the decision to turn back and began backing away down the passage. As I retreated, I saw them – eyes, eyes and more eyes – staring out from every poster, tracking my every move.

Exit 5.

'Yes!' I said, clenching my fist. Almost there. Only three more to go.

Riding the momentum of my small victory, I turned the corner.

The long white corridor stretched out again. Overhead: ↑ Exit 8.

'Dental Clinic . . . Escher Exhibit . . . Judicial Services . . . Beauty Clinic . . . High-Paying Part-time Jobs . . . Subway Manners . . .' I scanned the posters one by one. This time, all of them stared forwards. So I hadn't imagined it – those eyes *had* been watching me earlier. And if the eyes could move, what about the hands? What if they'd reached out and dragged me into the posters? A cold sweat ran down my spine. But the thought that I was getting closer to the end kept my legs moving.

'Salaryman . . . Security Camera . . .'

There didn't seem to be anything unusual with the salary-man. I finished checking the left-hand side and turned to inspect the opposite wall.

'Fire hydrant . . . door . . . door . . .'

As I was checking the one labelled 'Employees Only', my phone suddenly rang. In the silence of the underground passage, the sound echoed unnaturally loud.

I pulled out my smartphone. The black cat icon flashed across the screen. My ex.

Was it really her? Or just another anomaly?

I hesitated, staring at the icon. Then – abruptly – the ringtone cut off. If that had been the real her, I might've been able to tell her what was happening. Maybe she could've helped. More than that, I was worried. We'd lost contact so suddenly. What if she was sitting alone at the hospital, completely at a loss?

Anxious now, I hurried through the rest of the checks – doors, vents – until my phone rang again. The black cat icon. Another call from her.

I looked up. It was the ↑ Exit 8 sign. Was this call my lifeline – a single thread dangling down into hell? Or was it the edge of a bottomless swamp, waiting to drag me in?

It felt like the glowing yellow sign was testing me. I made up my mind and answered the phone.

'. . . Hello?' My voice trembled as I spoke.

'I finally got through. Where *are* you?'

It was her voice. No mistake. It was really her.

2 HER

She and I grew up in a small town by the sea.

We were classmates in elementary school – though, to be fair, there was only one class. Our homeroom teacher loved music and taught us how to play all kinds of instruments: classical guitar, piano, trombone. In junior high – now split into two classes – we started a band with a kid who had also gone to our elementary school. He played guitar, she handled bass and vocals, and I did drums and keyboard. His family ran a fishing tackle shop near the coast, and we used their warehouse as our practice studio. When we rolled up the shutters, the sea stretched out before our eyes. We played our instruments as if jamming with the waves, and during breaks we'd sit on the sand and eat rice balls his mother had made.

Even after starting high school, we kept the band going. We met up at the warehouse once a week, practising regularly, and even played small live gigs at a house near the next station over. After graduation, she got admitted to an art university in the Tokyo suburbs. I enrolled in a programming school in the city. He was the only one who stayed behind, helping out with the family shop. Naturally, the band broke up.

I'd never met my father. My mother worked as a nurse and raised me the best she could, but I often felt smothered by her dedication. I couldn't wait to live on my own. My girlfriend, on the other hand, clashed constantly with her parents, who only seemed to dote on her perfect, high-achieving older sister. She'd long dreamed of going to Tokyo and becoming a designer.

'Let's play music again sometime.' That's what he said when he came to see us off at the ferry terminal. I knew how he felt about her. And I knew it wouldn't happen. She and I had started dating just before graduation. We'd already decided to move into an apartment together in Tokyo. We never told him. And now, I deeply regret that.

My student life in Tokyo – those strange, suspended years – passed by in the blink of an eye. I was shy and not exactly personable, which made job hunting a challenge. I ended up drifting from one programming gig to another. I wasn't especially skilled, which made me just another replaceable cog in the machine.

Then, one day, a massive earthquake struck.

Trains and cars had all come to a halt. I walked two hours to get home. When I finally opened the door, she was sitting in the dark, staring silently at the TV.

'What's wrong?' I asked.

'Look . . .' she whispered, her voice trembling as she pointed at the screen.

It was our town, being swallowed by a huge tsunami. The school building we knew so well. The park. The candy shop and toy store we used to visit. The only convenience store in town. All of it devoured by the sea. Through the swirling mud and debris, I spotted a familiar sign. The tackle shop. And just for a second, the melody of one of our old songs drifted across my mind. I wrapped my arms around her trembling shoulders and held her close. We stayed there, in that dark room, watching image after image of our hometown being erased.

Thankfully, my mother and her family, who lived on higher ground, were safe. 'It's dangerous here. Stay in Tokyo for now,' they said. So we stayed. There was nothing we could do. The helplessness sank in day by day, thick as sediment.

Looking back now, we could have donated, even a little. We could have gone back to volunteer, even if just for a few days. But we didn't. We did *nothing*. We just stared at the unfolding tragedy from afar, dazed, like it was something happening in a different world entirely. And little by little, without even realising it, we abandoned it all – our town and our friend who'd gone missing.

And so, sometimes, I still imagine that maybe he's alive somewhere. Maybe one day, we'll bump into each other. He'll tap me on the shoulder in a subway car and say, 'Hey, what've you been up to? Still making music?'

And maybe we'll talk, just like old times. Maybe that day will come.

The following year, she got a job at a small publishing company in Tokyo, and we moved into a slightly larger apartment. We were still living together, but little by little, the conversations stopped. We talked a couple of times about whether we should get married – or break up. But neither of us could picture ourselves as good parents or imagine building a warm, loving home. And more than anything, the unspoken guilt we carried had started to weigh heavily on us. It felt like we weren't allowed to have a happy future. A few years ago, I'd caught that virus when it was going around, and ever since, I'd been dealing with chronic asthma. I still hadn't landed a full-time job – just drifting from one temp gig to the next. All of that only deepened my sense that I wasn't fit to be a parent. And now, all of a sudden, as I was being asked to make that choice, I found myself lost in a literal maze of confusion.

'I finally got through! Where are you?' Her voice came through the phone, full of relief. Of course she'd been worried – she'd just told me she was pregnant, and then I'd gone completely silent for so long.

'Sorry. . . I got a bit lost.'

I didn't know if she'd believe me, but I told her the truth anyway.

'Where are you now?'

'I don't know . . . I'm still underground.'

'Underground?'

'I've just been going in circles, unable to get out,' I replied while glancing sideways, scanning the metal doors and vents for signs of another anomaly.

'How's that possible?' she let out a small laugh.

'You know I've always been hopeless with directions.'

When we first moved to Tokyo, I was always getting lost, especially in big stations like Shinjuku and Shibuya. They were practically labyrinths to me. And every time, she was the one who helped me find the way.

'I think I'll be able to get out soon.'

Just then, as I turned to check behind the ↑ Exit 8 sign, the call went quiet. A long pause. Then, from her end of the line, I heard the faint sound of a baby's laughter.

I stopped at the corner and asked, 'What's wrong?'

'I don't know what to do . . .'

'Huh?'

'I can't decide.'

I couldn't breathe. Her words left me speechless.

'I feel so lost . . .'

I heard her sniffle, and beneath it, a baby's cry echoed faintly through the phone. Just imagining the weight of her struggle made my chest ache. And then, without meaning to, all the thoughts I'd been holding back came spilling out in a rush of messy words.

'This morning, on the subway . . . there was this woman holding a crying baby. And some guy started yelling at her.'

'Yeah?'

'No one did anything. Everyone just kept staring at their phones.'

'That's awful . . .'

'But I didn't do anything either. I pretended not to see. I got off the train like it wasn't my problem. And someone like that . . . someone like me . . . maybe I don't deserve to be a father.' As I kept talking, my voice began to falter. 'I've just felt so awful ever since seeing that happen . . . my head's been spinning.'

I thought back to that day. We watched our town being swallowed by the tsunami on TV – and did nothing. And now again today, turning away like I always do. Day after day, repeating the same thing. Looking away.

'I want to change . . .'

I said it aloud and began tearing up. My knees gave out and I sank to the floor at the corner.

'I want to get out of here . . .'

'Yeah . . .' She was crying too, on the other end of the line.

'I'll find the exit. I'll come to you as soon as I can!'

'I'll be waiting.'

She was waiting for me. Maybe we could finally change. Maybe we could finally break free from the loop we'd been stuck in and take our first step towards the future.

Encouraged to push forwards by her voice, I stood up and scanned everything in sight – the coin lockers, the blanket, the paper cup, the photo booth – then stepped to the corner and took a deep breath.

'Hold on a little longer. I'm coming,' I said, just before rounding the corner. On the other end of the line, the babies began to cry one after another, in a rising chorus of panic. Her voice began to distort, tangled in the wailing.

'I-I-I-I'll . . . wa-wa-wa-wait . . . ting-ting-ting . . .'

The words looped over and over, climbing in pitch until they became a sharp, metallic shriek – then stopped suddenly. I winced instinctively.

'Hello?' I called out hesitantly. But there was nothing. No crying. No hospital room. No sound at all. It was as if the call had never happened.

'Huh?'

Pulling the phone back from my ear, I looked at the screen. It was covered in yellow, as if someone had smeared thick paint across it.

'No . . .'

No, this couldn't be. I could barely breathe. My breaths turned shallow, erratic. I lifted my gaze to look at the signboard.

Exit 0.

A cold bead of sweat ran down my back.

'No, no, no . . .' The words came out in a feeble whisper. I looked at the phone again, two, three times.

Was the whole call an anomaly? Her words. Her tears. None of it real?

No – I couldn't accept that. I stared at the screen as if trying to burn through it with my eyes. But all I saw was that awful, sickly yellow.

I began to hyperventilate. This place was mocking me. The hope I'd just begun to feel. The possibility of reconciliation. My decision to become a father. All of it, erased like it had never mattered at all.

My teeth chattered uncontrollably. My knees buckled. I could barely walk. But if I didn't move forwards, I knew I'd lose my mind. Staggering, I turned the corner and faced the passageway once more. And then – I stopped breathing.

'Ah . . . ah . . .'

A pitiful groan slipped out, echoing through the corridor. The entire underground passage was soaked in yellow – the walls, the floor, the ceiling. Every inch of the space had been consumed by that sickly hue. And with it, the last threads of my sanity snapped.

'Aaaahhhh!!'

I clawed at my head, coughing violently. My stomach convulsed. Mucus surged up from my throat. I crumpled down and vomited into a nearby drain. Bits of this morning's convenience store sandwich and yoghurt were mixed in the bile, sloshing across the bright-yellow tiles.

I couldn't breathe. Gasping, I clutched at my throat and collapsed onto the floor. I had the terrifying sense that someone was watching me. I looked up. Through my blurring vision, I saw it: the ↑ Exit 8 sign, hanging from the ceiling, staring down at me.

I'm going to die here.

My retching worsened as waves of panic ripped through me.

I fumbled desperately through my backpack for my inhaler, but it wasn't there. In one frantic motion, I turned the entire bag upside down, dumping its contents across the yellow floor.

Scattered across the yellow floor were an empty water bottle, my power bank, glasses case, a few spare masks. Amid the mess, I spotted my inhaler. I grabbed it, shoved it into my mouth – and got nothing. Just a dry, rasping hiss.

'Gaahh!'

I hurled the spent inhaler down the corridor and began crawling back the way I came, dragging myself across the yellow tiles on my stomach. I had to get out before I lost my mind. I turned two corners before I reached the signboard.

Exit 1.

The number had gone up. Seeing it steadied me. I took a breath and pushed myself onto my feet.

'It's going to be fine,' I murmured to myself as I started walking slowly, deliberately, towards the next corner. That was all I could do; keep putting one foot in front of the other, no matter how long it took. Hours. Days. I didn't know, but I knew I would eventually reach Exit 8.

I found myself once again in that long white passageway, the familiar ↑ Exit 8 sign glowing overhead. But this time, there was someone standing beneath it – a young boy. He looked to be around five or six years old, dressed in a grimy blue T-shirt and denim shorts. His hair was tousled, lashes long, cheeks scratched with thin trails of blood seeping out. He stood perfectly still in the middle of the corridor, eyes locked on me in an alert gaze.

'An anomaly . . .'

There was no doubt in my mind. Without hesitation, I turned on my heel and started back the way I came.

Footsteps followed from behind. Unnerved, I quickened my pace. I didn't dare look back, terrified at the thought of what might happen next. I walked faster, turned the corner, and reached the signboard. This was supposed to be the 'safe zone', but I was still being pursued. What the hell was going on?

Then I saw the number.

Exit 0.

My eyes widened.

'What? Why?'

I had turned back because I'd seen an anomaly. That's what I was supposed to do. So why had the number gone down? I scrambled to read the information board.

Information
Do not overlook any anomalies.
If you find an anomaly, turn back immediately.
If you do not find any anomalies, do not turn back.
Go out through Exit 8.

'If you find an anomaly . . . turn back immediately . . .'

I traced the words with my finger and let out a gasp.

'So that wasn't . . . an anomaly?'

Sensing someone behind me, I turned round. It was the boy.

He looked at me timidly, the blood still dripping from his cheek. The smell of his sweat, faint and grassy, drifted through the sterile passage.

'Are you lost?' I asked, and he responded with a slight nod.

'Are you alone? Or is there someone with you?'

He didn't reply. Then, suddenly, he broke into a run. He bolted round the corner and vanished into the passageway.

Could there be someone else here? Clinging to the faintest thread of hope, I followed the boy.

When I turned the corner, I found myself again in that same long white passage. Overhead, the ↑ Exit 8 sign glowed as always. The boy stopped beneath it, raised his right arm parallel to the floor and pointed down the passage. I squinted, wondering who might appear. Just then, someone turned the far corner – it was that same salaryman.

'Oh, you mean that guy . . .' My shoulders slumped in disappointment. 'I mean . . . he's barely human . . .'

With a sigh, I looked back towards the approaching figure. But the boy was still pointing – steady, unmoved. What was he seeing? Was it possible we were seeing two different things? Was there something or somebody else there between the boy and the salaryman? As my thoughts raced, the salaryman drew closer with the same robotic stride, his expression blank, and passed us without a word.

3 THE WALKING MAN

Goddamn it. How the hell did I end up in this mess?

I keep walking in goddamn circles. What the hell is this place? 'Information?' 'Find anomalies?' 'Go out through Exit 8?' Yeah? Screw that. What kind of joke is this? Some twisted game for rich bastards to watch and laugh at from their penthouses?

I don't have time for this shit. Not today. I have somewhere important to be. I'm in a hurry. And just my luck, today of all days, I get trapped in this freakshow. This goddamn place doesn't even have signal. I gotta get out of here.

And don't even get me started on these so-called anomalies. Makes my skin crawl. Blood dripping from the ceiling. Flickering lights. Some freak in a three-piece suit sprinting towards me out of nowhere. Gimme a goddamn break.

Still, I'll say this – I'd rather *have* anomalies than not. It's when nothing happens that I start losing my goddamn mind. When everything *seems* normal but feels just a little off – that's when it really eats away at you. Like earlier. I didn't see a single damn anomaly, so I went ahead . . . and got booted back to Exit 0. I lost it. Where the hell was the anomaly?

And as if I wasn't already screwed enough, I run into this lost kid. No clue how he ended up here. Wandering alone. Couldn't just leave him, right? So I started taking him along. But man, what a piece of work. Doesn't talk, walks slow as hell, total dead weight. Like I needed *that* on top of everything else.

But, believe it or not, my luck started turning. Since I had to slow down for the kid, I actually started noticing more anomalies. Like posters that were getting gradu-ally bigger, or signboards hanging upside down. Subtle stuff, but I caught it. And just now, I gambled on a 'no anomaly' passage – and it paid off. Made it all the way to Exit 4. Hell yeah.

All right, next hallway. Let's go. Anomalies, anoma-lies . . .

↑ Exit 8 sign? Check. Vent? Check. Doors: Electrical Room, Employees Only, Terminal Test Valve Room, fire hydrant – nothing. All clear. Good.

Oh, and here she comes again. That same high-school girl. Short skirt, oversized cardigan, jangly charms on her school bag. Every time I try to say something, check if she's okay, she ignores me. Just marches forwards, face like a goddamn Noh mask. No emotion. Not even sure she's human. Maybe a robot. Maybe some kind of AI. Freaks me the hell out. Still, gotta check her for anomalies too.

And then up next are the posters. 1, 2, 3, 4, 5, 6 and the security camera sign. Let's call that 7 . . . looks good. Turn the corner. The homeless guy's nasty pile of rubbish and the photo booth – no anomalies.

This kid, though – man. He's *not* helping. I'm busting my ass out here, trying to survive, and he doesn't even *try* to help look for anomalies. Hey, kid. You see anything? What the hell is that look for? I'm trying to work *with* you here. You could at least say something. Hey, don't start getting all scared and shit. I'm being *nice*, okay? C'mon now, stop scowling at me. All right, all right. No need to frown like that. Sorry if I scared you, okay? Jeez. Wait – why the hell am *I* apologising? I even gave a fake smile. Me. Smiling. I don't do shit like that. My ex-wife used to say it all the time – *I've given up on you, but at least try to be nicer to our child.* And today's the day I'm supposed to meet him. So fine. I'll treat this like practice.

I turn the corner. Exit 5! Yes, yes, yes! Just three more to go. I've got this far, now I can't screw this up.

↑ Exit 8, vents, check. How 'bout the posters and sign? 1, 2, 3, 4, 5, 6, 7 . . . wait, something off? 1, 2, 3, 4, 5, 6 and 7. No, they're fine, No anomalies. High-school girl . . . check. Electrical Room, Employees Only, Terminal Test Valve Room, fire hydrant . . . all clear! All right, let's go. Lockers . . . wait, where the hell is the kid?

I glance around. There he is, already turning the corner. Hey, wait! Shit! What if there was an anomaly? But nope, there he is, standing right in front of the sign. Hm? Wait a second . . . no way. Exit 6? Yes! Good going, kiddo. I ruffle his hair, but he looks annoyed. No manners, this one. But whatever. Just two more to go. Let's go. ↑ Exit 8, vents. Okay. Posters: 1, 2, 3, 4, 5, 6 – huh? The schoolgirl behind me just stopped walking.

'Excuse me, but . . .'

What the – she's talking now? After ignoring me this whole time?

'Are you lost too?'

So she *can* speak. Finally asking for help, huh? I shoot her a fake smile, and she actually smiles back.

'I can't seem to get out of here. Would you mind if I came with you?'

Of course I say yes. She's stuck in here too, same as us. I introduce her to the kid, but she doesn't even look at him. And now the kid's glaring at her. Come on, you two. Try getting along.

Posters: 1, 2, 3, 4, 5, 6, and 7. Gotta stay sharp for anomalies, quick. I take a glance at the girl. What's she doing now? She's staring hard and poking at the Beauty Clinic and High-Paying Part-Time Jobs poster. Clearly she has no intention of doing this properly. Useless. I'm about to snap when she turns to me and says, 'What *is* this place, anyway?'

Hell if I know. If I *did*, we'd be out of here already.

'You think we're already . . . dead?'

Suddenly she's talking to me like I'm her friend or something. I don't even know how to respond. What the hell was she going on about?

'Maybe this is hell? Or purgatory?' she keeps going.

'Maybe we're stuck here 'cause we did something bad. We were learning about it in school – Dante's *Divine Comedy*? Purgatory's like this place between heaven and hell, where sinners wait for judgement while suffering.'

Purgatory? What is she even talking about? Sounds like one of those swirling spiral tower drawings I've seen before. But in a Japanese underground passage? Come on. That's too surreal even for this place.

Then she leans in a little, like she's trying to read my soul or something.

'Did you do something you feel guilty about?'

I mean . . . sure, I've got stuff. Who doesn't? Then – *bam!* – she slaps me on the chest and bursts out laughing. 'I'm kidding!'

What the hell is wrong with this girl?

'It's just a never-ending passageway. Let's hurry up and find the anomalies.'

She's pissing me off, but I keep it together. Be the adult, right? Smile. Just smile. Smile harder when you're pissed – that's what I learned. I tell her, real polite-like, that I don't see anything unusual, so we should move ahead. But she doesn't follow. Just stands there. What now?

'There's always someone who comes walking from that direction,' she says, staring down the passage.

Was she talking about herself?

'You know, the man. That creepy one.'

. . . The hell?

'This time he's not coming. Maybe that's the anomaly.'

Wait. *What?* She couldn't be talking about – me? I feel a chill crawl up my neck.

And then she's suddenly *right there*, in front of me.

'Don't you think it's better here?' she murmurs, brushing her fingers along my face. Her eyes fixed on me, like she's trying to draw me in. What's she trying to do?

'Every day, you cram onto a packed train, go to work, repeat the same thing again and again. That sounds more like hell. Poor thing.'

What is she on about? I try to keep listening, but I can feel my face twitching.

'Every day, you cram onto a packed train, go to work, repeat the same thing again and again. That sounds more like hell. Poor thing.'

Huh?

'Every day, you cram onto a packed train, go to work, repeat the same thing again and again. That sounds more like hell. Poor thing.'

She keeps repeating it. Over and over. What the hell is this? And the kid – what the hell's with him now? He's tugging at my sleeve.

'Every day, you cram onto a packed train, go to work, repeat the same thing again and again. That sounds more like he—'

Suddenly, she stops. I lean in to check. A creepy smile is plastered across her face. She's totally still, like a mannequin. I step closer. She's not even breathing. Is she dead?

'Hey,' I say, waving a hand in front of her. Then her eyes snap open and she starts to shout.

'Sounds more like hell! Poor thing!!'

What? That voice, I've heard it somewhere.

'Every day, you cram onto a packed train, go to work, repeat the same thing again and again! That sounds more like hell! Poor thing!!'

Wait, that's *my* voice. What the hell is happening here? She keeps shouting over and over, in my voice, and the kid turns ghost-white. That's an anomaly. Definitely. I grab his hand and yank him backwards, sprinting down the corridor. She just keeps screaming in my voice the whole way.

We turn the corner and the voice cuts off. I feel sick. I need to get out of here. Now. Before something worse shows up. The signboard reads Exit 7. Just one more to go. I catch my breath and turn the corner.

Not long now, just gotta get past this last stretch. I glance up: ↑ Exit 8, check. Vents, check. Posters . . . 1, 2, 3, 4, 5 – and there she was. The high-school girl. Just passing by, expressionless. Like none of that ever happened. What the hell is wrong with her? Scaring me like that, like some possessed freak. Monster. But what if I end up like her? Posters 6, 7. Hell no – I'd rather die. Door, door, door. No anomalies, all clear.

Hurry, c'mon, I say to the kid, pulling him forwards, but he won't budge. He's just standing there, frozen in front of the Employees Only door. God, this kid. Always in the way. Hey, it's fine, let's go. Goddammit! I need to get outta here quick. I yank his arm hard, dragging him off the spot. Locker, rubbish, photo booth . . . all good. Exit 8 – next! This is it!

Wait. No. No! Everything goes white. My vision blurs.

How is it back to 0? How?! Back to the damn beginning?! Again?! How many times are they gonna do this?!

My scream echoes through the passage. Why didn't you look properly, I glare at the kid. Goddamn brat. Boiling with rage, I kick the Exit 0 sign. Don't get angry. Don't lash out. That's why I got kicked out of the house. That's why I can't see my wife. Can't see my son. Hold it together. Breathe. But the more I try to tell myself that, the more the blood surges to my head, and I can't stop it.

I glance at the Information sign on the side.

Do not overlook any anomalies. That one line makes my rage explode again. Anomalies, my ass! I lunge at the sign, rip it from the wall and hurl it to the floor. This thing. This damn thing – it's the one screwing everything up! I stomp on it again and again, over and over. Damn it! Damn it! Goddamn it! I was supposed to see my son today!

When I turn round, the kid is standing there, staring at me from a distance, frozen. That look on his face, it's the same look my son used to give me. Back when I used to lose my temper. Back when I drank too much. I saw a doctor. I got help. I gave up drinking. I thought I had changed. So why the hell am I still like this?

Let's go, I mutter, yanking the kid's arm as we turn the corner.

Then I stop. Ahead of us is a stairwell leading up to the surface. Is that . . . an exit? I hear the sound of traffic. Leaves rustling in the wind. Birds singing. Sunlight streams down the stairwell.

It . . . has to be the outside. My voice trembles with excitement. It feels like I haven't seen sunlight in decades. So that sign . . . that 'information' was bullshit after all. I was an idiot to fall for it. I grab the kid's hand and start up the stairs, but he resists, pulling against me, trying to drag me back down.

What the hell is wrong with you? It's the exit, can't you see? It's right there! I shake him off in frustration, and he tumbles down the stairs.

Shit. What have I done?

My blood runs cold. I look down and see him curled up at the bottom. He lets out a groan, then lifts his head to glare at me. There's blood running down his scraped cheek.

C'mon, let's go kid . . . I say as I reach out, my voice unsteady. Let's get out of here together. But the kid just stares at me, motionless, blood running down his forehead. He's not going to come. I can't take him with me. That's it. I have to leave him. He looks at me piercingly with his black eyes. Can I really abandon a kid this small here?

'My son's waiting . . .'

I tear my eyes away and bolt up the stairs.

'I did everything I can. It's not my fault,' I mutter, taking long strides to outrun the feeling. My son's waiting. I still have child support to pay. I can't just rot and die in a place like this.

'I'm getting out . . .'

At the top of the stairs, the sky opens up. Bright blue. White clouds. A bird, then another, soars past them.

'I'm getting out . . . I'm getting out . . .'

Golden sunlight spills over me from between the clouds. It feels so good. Like I've been forgiven by God. Like I've been set free. Tears well up and fall down my cheeks.

'It's not my fault . . . it's not my fault . . .' the words tumble out.

'Not my fault . . . not my fault . . . it's not my fault.'

Those were the words I used to scream at my son every time I lost control.

4 THE BOY

My cheek burns, like it's on fire. I touch it, and my finger comes away red. I think I hurt my cheek when I fell down the stairs. It didn't hurt at all before, but when I saw the blood, it started to sting. Where did the big man go?

Up the stairs, I saw the sky. It was so blue. White clouds floated like balloons. Birds flew through the air, free and easy. I could hear people walking and talking. Cars. Trains. But that was all an anomaly.

The big man went out through the fake exit.

I waited at the bottom of the stairs for a while, but he never came back. So I turned round and started walking the way we came. Left at the wall. Then right.

There it was: the sign for Exit 1.

I knew it. That exit from earlier was a fake. What's going to happen to the man who left through it?

I turn the corner and there it is – the long straight hallway. How many times have I gone round and round this place? Now I'm all alone. And that makes it even scarier.

But then, from the far end of the passage, someone turns the corner. It's him! The big man.

'Mister!'

I start running towards him. He's walking in my direction.

'Mister?'

I call out again, right in front of him, but it's like he can't see me. He's looking forwards and just keeps walking.

I scramble out of the way. He keeps walking straight ahead and starts to turn the corner.

'Mister, it's me!'

I grab his arm and pull hard, but he won't stop. He won't even look at me. He keeps walking, dragging me along behind him, then suddenly he freezes.

'Mister? What's wrong?'

I look up at his face. He's staring at his phone.

'Mister! Hey, mister!'

I tap his stomach again and again, but he doesn't move – he just keeps looking at his screen. Has he forgotten about me? Or maybe he wasn't the same person anymore. I wanted to help him. Now I don't know how.

'Aaaahhhh!!'

A man's scream echoes from far away. I flinch and hold my breath. Footsteps are getting closer. Someone's coming. I get scared and run.

'It's going to be fine,' a man's voice calls out. The footsteps are getting louder too. I run into the usual long, straight passage and look back.

At the far end of the hall, someone turns the corner. It's a young man.

Who is he?

I stare at him. He looks back and mutters, 'An anomaly.' Then he turns round and starts to leave.

'Don't go!'

I chase after him. I run, turn left and then right. I catch up just as he stops in front of the Exit 0 sign, tilting his head.

'So that wasn't . . . an anomaly?'

He looks at the Information sign, and then at me.

'Are you lost?' he asks.

I nod nervously.

'Are you alone? Or is there someone with you?'

I don't know how to answer, so I run again.

I return to the usual passage.

The man – the big one – was coming towards us from the other end. I point at him. Maybe this younger man could help him. But he looks surprised.

'Oh, you mean that guy . . .'

The younger man seems to recognise him. But then he gives a little shake of his head, like he's given up.

'I mean . . . he's barely human . . .'

Barely human? But just a little while ago, he was human.

He went up the fake exit stairwell, so maybe now he wasn't human anymore. I'm scared, and I keep watching his back as he walks away.

'Let's go,' the young man calls to me, and starts walking ahead.

That's when I notice the ↑ Exit 8 sign. The words, 'Go Back Go Back Go Back Go Back' are written behind it. That's an anomaly. I run after the young man and turn the corner.

'Lockers . . . bedding . . . photo booth . . .'

The young man searches more carefully than the big man did. I need to tell him about what I saw. But for some reason, I'm scared to say it. Before I can speak, he's already moving on.

'Where's the anomaly . . .?' he murmurs.

He turns the corner, and when he sees the Exit 0 sign he looks really disappointed.

I want to say I'm sorry for not telling him sooner. But before I can open my mouth, he smiles at me and says, 'It'll be okay.' His smile looks tired. He's probably been lost here for a long time, too.

I walk beside him and we turn the corner.

It's that same long, straight passage again. The yellow ↑ Exit 8 sign is still there.

'↑ Exit 8 sign . . . Dental Clinic . . . Escher Exhibit . . . Judicial Services . . . Beauty Clinic . . . High-Paying Part-time Jobs . . . Subway Manners . . . Security Cameras in Operation . . .' He points at each one, checking for anomalies. Then, something catches his eye. He stops in front of the Escher poster.

'This one . . .'

He stares hard at the drawing. It's an ∞ symbol with ants walking on it. A strange and interesting picture.

'The Möbius strip . . . is it facing the wrong way . . .?'

He traces the ∞ symbol again and again with his finger.

'Is it an anomaly? Or . . . is it the same as before?'

He keeps muttering to himself, so I decide to leave him behind and walk ahead.

'Wait! I think . . . this might be an anomaly!' I hear his voice calling out behind me, but I just keep walking.

'Aw, come on!'

He comes running after me. I speed up so he won't catch up, turning left, then right.

'Damn it . . . we have to start over again . . .' he sighs as he turns the corner. But then he stops and lets out a small, 'Oh.'

It's because I'm standing right in front of the Exit 1 sign.

'Sorry . . . Guess that wasn't an anomaly after all,' he says, awkwardly.

He's just like the big man. Always afraid of anomalies. So scared he starts doubting whether something is one or not, and then he gets it wrong.

We turn the corner together, and it's the usual straight passage. The young man searches carefully for anomalies.

'Doesn't look like there's anything,' he says, starting to walk on. But I stay still, staring at the door.

'What is it?' he asks, noticing I haven't moved. He walks back towards me. Then he sees it – the strange doorknob right in the middle.

従業員専用

'*Ah, the doorknob . . .*'

He stares at it and says, 'It's an anomaly. Let's go back.'

We turn the corner and find the Exit 2 sign. He looks a little embarrassed, but smiles at me. 'Thanks, you did well.'

I feel happy and sniffle a little. That's a habit I really need to fix – Mum always scolds me about it. But when I get happy I just end up doing it.

'All right, let's keep going.' We turn the corner together.

It's the same straight passage again. But something's different.

The yellow Exit 8 sign is slowly blinking – glowing and dimming like a firefly.

Just as he says, 'An anomaly . . .' the lights flicker and go out completely. It's pitch dark, with only the ↑ Exit 8 sign still glowing.

Clang! A loud noise echoes through the tunnel, and the man swings his phone light towards it. The cover of an air duct had come loose and crashed to the floor. It's covered with blood. It's gross. I hear tiny footsteps skittering along the walls, and babies crying from somewhere far off.

Then comes a piercing, high-pitched tone. I clamp my hands over my ears. It isn't loud, but it really bothers me. In the dark, I remember something.

'What's that noise? It's small, but it hurts my ears.' I'd asked Mummy that once, when we went to a pizza place underground.

'It's a sound to keep rodents away,' she told me. 'Humans can barely hear it, but for rats, it's really loud and horrible.'

That sharp sound brought her words back to me. I wonder what Mummy's doing now. Is she looking for me? It's so dark. And so scary.

I thought I heard Mummy's voice in the dark, saying, 'Goodnight.' She always stroked my head after turning off the lights, once I was tucked into bed. I really want to see Mummy.

A screeching noise comes from somewhere above. The man slowly raises the light from his phone. There, on the glowing ↑ Exit 8 sign, is a swarm of mice. They're clinging to it like cockroaches, all huddled together and staring straight at us.

'What the hell . . .' the man mutters.

He shines his light directly at one of the mice. It has a human ear growing out of its body. The one next to it has a human nose. And the mouse on top has an eyeball stuck to its back.

'What a horrible thing to do,' Mummy had said the other day while looking at the news on her phone. There'd been a mouse used in some experiment to grow a human ear. It was inside a glass case, with an ear stuck right in the middle of its body. 'Humans do terrible things,' Mummy always said, her face full of sadness as she scrolled. But she'd soon look away and forget all about it. If I did something bad, though, she'd get really mad.

Drawn by the yellow glow of the sign, the mice begin to gather — ones with ears, ones with noses, ones with eyes. From the middle of the wriggling swarm, I hear a baby crying. The man turns his light towards the sound. It's a mouse with a human mouth. Its lips move, and the baby's wailing comes out of it. Its teeth are black and broken, like they are rotting. Suddenly, it lets out a piercing scream. The man jumps, dropping his phone. The light vanishes, and everything goes dark. All around us come the jumbled sounds of mice squeaking and the baby crying.

'This way!' the man says, grabbing my hand and pulling me back the way we came. One baby cry becomes two, then more — they are getting closer. The fluorescent lights of the sign flicker, then go out. I can see them, mice, clinging to the walls. Every one of them has human ears, noses, eyes or mouths.

When we turn a corner, the lights flick on again. The baby cries stop and the mice disappear. Even the high-pitched anti-rodent sound has gone. I turn back slowly. The mice have vanished. In front of us is the Exit 3 sign.

The young man is having a coughing fit. He can't stop. He looks like he is in pain, wheezing and gasping for air. Maybe he has asthma. There were kids in my preschool who had asthma too, because of some kind of bad virus. They always seemed to be coughing.

The man breathes in, then out, slow and steady, to calm down. Then he takes my hand and we turn the corner.

It's the usual passageway. The same yellow ↑ Exit 8 sign.

Under the sign, there's a black cat. It lets out a soft meow.

'Pepper?' I say the name out loud. That's our cat. Why is he here?

Pepper is sitting under the yellow sign, all curled up. He meows again, then stands and walks towards us, across the white floor. When he gets to my feet, he meows again. I know it now – it's definitely Pepper. As I pet his head, I feel like someone's calling me.

I look up the passageway. Right where Pepper had been, there's now a lady standing. She's wearing a white dress. Who is that? The man next to me is just staring at her. Not moving at all. I rub my eyes and look closer.

'Mummy?' My voice comes out squeaky.

Why is she here? I rub my eyes again. I look again. She's looking right at me. She looks sad. Maybe she's been looking for me this whole time, ever since I got lost.

'Mummy . . . I'm sorry.'

A single tear falls from her eyes. I knew it. I was right. The woman standing under the yellow sign . . . that's my mum.

5 Sin

'Mummy?' the boy murmured beside me.

'Mummy . . . I'm sorry.' He kept speaking to the anomaly standing at the end of the passage. She wore a white dress, tears spilling from her eyes as she gazed at the boy with what looked like affection.

'That's your . . . mum?' I asked, hesitantly. He nodded.

I swallowed hard. Because to me, that same figure looked like my ex. A wave of fear washed over me. To him, she appeared as his mother. To me, as someone I care about deeply. Then I remembered the fake phone call.

This place – this underground passage – toyed with the mind. It exploited your soft spots. Dragged your guilt out into the open. Forced you to replay it. To confront it. To repent. It was like some kind of twisted self-reflection programme.

I looked up at the glowing ↑ Exit 8 sign on the ceiling. She was still standing beneath it, silently watching us.

'What do we do?' I saw her lips move, far away, but her voice echoed in my ear, like a phone call. She had asked me that question that very morning. *What do we do about the baby?* It had been circling in my head ever since I started wandering through these halls. And now the anomaly was asking it again.

'Mummy!' Suddenly, the boy broke into a run. I lunged after him and grabbed his hand.

'Don't go to her!'

I pulled him back and wrapped him in my arms. His tiny heart was beating wildly against my chest. What would have happened if he'd reached her, if he had walked straight into that anomaly? Would he have ended up like that salaryman, wandering these tunnels as a lifeless puppet with no emotion left?

'Mummy! Mummy!' The boy struggled in my arms, trying to break free and run to her.

'Stop! That's not your mum!' I forced his face towards mine. His eyes flew wide open, staring at me with a look that said, *How could you say something so awful?*

'That's not your mum,' I said firmly. 'She looks like someone else to me.' I tried to reason with him, pressing on.

'What do we do?' It was her voice again, impossibly close. Was he hearing it too? He thrashed wildly in my arms, trying everything he could to reach her.

'Mummy, I'm sorry! I'm sorry!' He screamed like someone possessed – no longer the calm, quiet child from before.

'I'm sorry! I'm sorry! I'm sorry!' His body convulsed with the words. His nose began to bleed. Then his eyes rolled back, and he lost consciousness. He collapsed against me, limp. And the anomaly, still wearing the shape of my ex, stood watching, its empty, unreadable eyes stayed locked on the boy. Then they shifted to me. Slowly, the figure raised a hand and placed it on its belly.

'What do we do?' it asked again. And just as the words reached my ears, I heard a faint thump-thump, like the heartbeat of something small inside her. It matched the rhythm of the boy's heartbeat against my chest.

'Stop it . . .'

My breath grew ragged, and a cough rose up in my throat. I scooped the boy up in my arms and staggered backwards down the passage. At the corner, I glanced back one last time.

The lips of the anomaly moved slowly. *I'll be waiting.* Her voice echoed in my ears.

I sat down beneath the Exit 4 sign, the boy's head resting on my lap as he continued to sleep. I watched him quietly. Where had he come from? How had he ended up in this place? I remembered the way he had screamed *I'm sorry* again and again. If this place truly existed to make people reflect on their sins, then perhaps he, too, had done something – something he believed had hurt his mother. As I turned that thought over in my mind, I heard a faint cough. The boy's eyes fluttered open.

'Are you all right?'

He looked confused, like he didn't know what had just happened. He stared blankly up at the ceiling for a while, then slowly pushed himself up, glancing around.

'Thank goodness.'

Without saying anything, he sat down beside me. He leaned back against the wall and lowered his head.

'Did you . . . get separated from your mum?' I asked.

He didn't reply. He reached up and touched his nose. There was still a smear of blood beneath it. I wiped it off with my sleeve.

Then, in a tiny voice, he murmured, 'It was on purpose . . .'

'Huh?'

'I got lost . . . on purpose.'

'Why?'

'I wanted Mummy to come and find me.'

That was probably it. That was his one and only sin. And maybe it was that small act that had made the anomaly appear in the shape of his mother. He looked up at me like a frightened kitten. Did he think I'd be angry? I met his gaze and gave him a smile.

'Hey, I've done this same thing, you know,' I said. 'Got lost on purpose. I just wanted my mum to come looking for me.' As I shared the memory with a laugh, I saw the corners of his mouth lift, just a little. His expression softened.

'Is your mummy scary?'

'She's scary when she's mad,' he replied.

'How about your dad?'

'I've never met him.'

'I see . . . same here.'

By the time I was born, my father was already gone. I never knew if he had left us or if he'd passed away. My mother never said a word about him.

'Mum, what was Dad like?' I'd asked once, when I was around the boy's age.

'I don't remember,' she had murmured after a long silence, like a single drop of water falling from a tap. And I remember thinking then, if she couldn't remember, maybe it was the same as him never having existed at all. After that, living with just my mum no longer felt strange. It became natural.

But when I started living with my ex and thinking seriously about building a family, I started feeling uneasy about my past. Could someone who had never known a father become one?

I looked at the boy next to me, his head still bowed. I used to do the same – getting lost on purpose just so my mother would come looking for me. And she always did. She would search everywhere, desperately. When she found me waiting at a police station, she'd scoop me up into a tearful hug. And in that moment, I'd know I was loved. It was a selfish, even cruel way to test her love. But she never once got angry at me.

My first memory of sin is the tearful face my mother made when she found me.

'We should get you back to your mum,' I said, ruffling the boy's hair. His crown was damp with sweat, and a faint, grassy scent rose from it. I planted my hands on the floor and stood up. 'All right, let's go,' I said. Together, we rounded the corner.

The long white underground passage stretched out before us. Overhead, the yellow ↑ Exit 8 sign glowed steadily.

'Dental Clinic . . . Escher Exhibit . . . Judicial Services . . . Beauty Clinic . . . High-Paying Part-time Jobs . . . Subway Manners . . .'

I checked each poster on the left-hand wall one by one, then shifted my gaze to the salaryman passing by, scanning him carefully for any sign of an anomaly.

'Salaryman . . . no anomalies . . .' I muttered under my breath as I watched his receding figure, then turned to face forwards again.

'Wait, where's the boy?' My own voice echoed down the empty corridor, flat and uneasy. The boy who had been walking right beside me was suddenly nowhere to be seen.

'Where'd you go?'

I spun round in a panic and rushed to the corner at the end of the passage. But the hallway beyond was completely deserted, lined only with neatly ordered lockers. Had he gone ahead on his own? I sighed, frustrated – I hadn't even finished checking for anomalies. Just then, the curtain of the photo booth twitched slightly. I crept closer, then yanked the curtain open.

'Hide and seek!'

The boy was sitting on the small seat inside, his eyes gleaming with mischief.

'Don't scare me like that!'

I let out a long breath, shoulders loosening as a smile broke across my face. Maybe he was starting to warm up to me. But before I could say anything else, I heard wheezing and a dry asthmatic cough, coming from somewhere nearby. Startled, I turned towards the sound. The pile of blankets stacked between the coin lockers and the photo booth were bulging in the shape of a person.

I hesitated, then slowly approached. The pile quivered with every fit of coughing. Each breath from under the blanket came out in a strained, wheezing rasp. Then I felt it in my own chest, as if it were contagious. I coughed, once, then again. From under the blanket came a rattling wheeze, followed by another round of deep coughing.

'Are you all right?' I asked, my own voice hoarse.

There was a muffled reply from beneath the layers.

'That virus . . .'

'Virus?'

'It . . . got me . . . since then . . . I . . .'

The coughing swallowed half his words. Broken and scattered. I knew the feeling. A few years ago, I caught that new virus that was going around. A high fever took me out for days. I was bedridden, barely able to breathe.

My airways had always been weak, which made my coughs especially violent. Even after the fever broke, the coughing remained. Ever since, I'd been living with asthma-like symptoms that never quite went away.

'So,' the old man said, 'what do you think? Am I an anomaly . . . or not?' His question made me instinctively lean forwards and peek beneath the pile of blankets. What I saw was an old man, his face caked with dried mud, his long, tangled hair knotted into clumps. Beneath a matted fringe, his eyes were clouded over, pale and unblinking, and they were fixed directly on me.

'Did I appear here just now,' he asked slowly, 'or have I been here all along?'

The way he said it made me feel like he really had been here from the start – that he wasn't an anomaly after all. Maybe I simply hadn't noticed him until now.

'Where . . . where are we?' I asked, pressing him as though he were the keeper of this strange place. 'How do we get out of here?'

'You'll just have to keep proving it. The devil's proof,' he said.

The words hit me sideways. I was left speechless.

'The scariest thing,' he went on, 'is when you can't prove it. Are there anomalies . . . or no anomalies . . . is there an Exit 8 . . . or is there not . . .'

He was right. When there was nothing to see, no 'anomaly' to point to, it became harder and harder to trust my own senses. Everything began to feel suspicious. Anything could be an anomaly.

'Why did you come here?' he asked suddenly.

'I . . . I don't know,' I replied, my voice cracking.

'You do know,' he said.

His bony hand reached out, clutching a paper cup from some chain coffee shop.

'This,' he said, 'is your sin.'

Dread crept up my spine as I leaned in to look.

Something red writhed inside the cup. I heard it – a faint sound: a baby's cry, drifting up from the bottom. The old man grabbed my arm and yanked it forwards, shoving the cup right in front of my face. Inside were tiny blood-soaked fingers. Ragged fingernails. Wisps of thin hair. They floated slowly, turning like laundry in a washing machine, swirling round and round in thick red liquid. They looked like the shredded remains of a baby. The colour drained from my face.

'The passage is showing you your sins . . . that's what the anomalies are . . .'

The homeless man broke into a violent cough – and from within the cup, the baby's scream rang out even louder. My knees gave out. Coughing, I stumbled backwards. That's when I caught a glimpse of the mirror fixed to the side of the photo booth. I couldn't believe what I saw. It wasn't me reflected there – it was the old man.

'Aaah!'

Without thinking, I grabbed my phone and smashed it against the mirror. The glass split into two jagged panes. One reflected my face, the other the old man's. From inside the mirror, his reflection spoke to me.

'You killed the baby . . .'

'No!'

'You abandoned it . . .'

'I was abandoned too! My dad left me!' As I shouted back – my raw, buried feelings rising to the surface – the baby's screaming intensified in my ears. I struck the mirror again and again, trying to shatter the nightmare. Fractures spread across the glass like spiderwebs, flickering between my reflection and the old man's.

'You'll never change . . . You'll never escape this place . . .' His cloudy eyes bore into mine. 'I . . . am your future.'

My stomach churned. I trembled violently. Blood was running down my hand, but I couldn't stop hitting the mirror. Then – someone grabbed my hand. I froze and looked up. It was the boy. I snapped back to reality. Shards of mirror lay scattered across the floor, and in them, I saw my own pale face staring back. I turned to the blankets. The man was gone. Only dirty cardboards and an empty paper cup remained. The boy gently tugged my still-quivering hand and began leading me back through the passage.

Just before we rounded the final corner into the safe zone, I heard coughing echo faintly in the distance.

In front of the Exit 5 sign, I slumped down, still shaking. The boy patted my back in silence. The back of my hand throbbed, cut by a shard of glass.

'It's okay . . . it's okay . . .' he whispered, over and over, like a spell.

I remembered how my mother used to do the same when I cried – whispering, 'It's okay, it's okay,' while gently rubbing my back.

'I'm sorry . . . I . . .'

Little by little, the trembling in my body subsided. The warmth of the boy's small palm brought me back to myself. He took my hand, still bleeding, and led me round the corner. The same long white passage stretched ahead.

'To Exit 8 . . .'

As I pointed up towards the glowing yellow ↑ Exit 8 sign, I heard the boy gently correct me.

'It's upside down.'

'Upside down?'

I squinted at the sign, and sure enough, the number '8' was inverted.

'You're right . . . It's flipped.'

It was as if the sign was mocking us.

We turned round, away from the anomaly, and came face-to-face with the Exit 6 sign.

'Just two more to go.'

With fresh momentum, we rounded the next corner and entered the same long white passage.

'To Exit 8,' I murmured, pointing up again at the glowing yellow sign above.

'Let's go!' the boy replied brightly. For the first time, he was actively helping me search for anomalies. I couldn't help but smile. We began pointing at the posters together.

'Dental Clinic . . . Escher Exhibit . . . Judicial Services . . .'

'All clear!' the boy called out, then pointed at the salaryman approaching from ahead.

'Big man!'

'All clear,' I replied.

'Beauty Clinic . . . High-Paying Part-time Jobs . . . Subway Manners . . .'

We kept walking, calling them out together. Then, suddenly, a loud creaking sound echoed from behind us. We turned round. The Employees Only door was slowly opening. It creaked as it moved, stopping halfway. I'd tried pushing and pulling it earlier, but it hadn't budged. So why was it opening now? Was it another anomaly? Or was someone actually inside? I crept towards the door without making a sound and, gripping the knob, gave it a push. Inside was pitch black.

'Uh . . . hello?'

My voice echoed back at me, making it clear the space inside was much larger than expected. I listened carefully. A steady sound emerged from the darkness. It sounded like . . . a train? I narrowed my eyes. Through the inky black, I spotted the faint glow of a train window.

'The subway?'

And inside that train – I saw *myself*. 'I' was wearing earphones, holding my phone, staring blankly out the window. Then, a baby started crying. A sharp, piercing wail echoed in the darkness like a plea for help. The me inside the train took off his earphones and looked towards the crying. And then came a man's voice, shouting, 'Shut that thing up!' The baby screamed louder.

For a moment, 'I' stared towards them. Then, without a word, I put the earphones back in. And just like that, all the sound vanished. The train's rumbling, the shouting, the crying – everything was swallowed into silence. Like the void of space.

That was unmistakably me.

The me in the train gazed out the window into pure darkness. And in that soundless world, our eyes met. The eyes I saw staring back were hollow. The kind that belonged to someone who had spent his days numbly going through the motions, wilfully ignoring everything uncomfortable.

'I'd always turned a blind eye . . .' I whispered, my voice trembling. The boy looked up at me, worried. 'Now this place is making me watch it . . .'

I closed the door slowly, its hinges creaking, then turned back the way we'd come and rounded the corner.

'What's the first thing you'll do if we get out of here?' I asked the boy as he stared up at the sign for Exit 7. Just one more until Exit 8.

'Pizza.'

'Pizza?'

'I wanna eat pizza with lots of cheese.'

His answer caught me off guard. But maybe that's all there really is. Maybe when you finally escape, your wants are that simple. I asked myself again – *do I even want to leave this place?* Even if I make it out through Exit 8, won't I just end up repeating everything all over again? Living each day with guilt, averting my eyes from the things I don't want to face. Is that the life I want to return to?

'I don't know anymore . . .' I gave the boy a weak smile as I said it. The dull ache in my wounded hand seemed to spread to my chest.

'I feel like . . . even if I go back, things still won't go right.' I said it aloud – the fear I hadn't admitted to anyone.

If I returned to the world, to the clinic where my ex was waiting . . . what should I do? Could I really live up to it – be the man she needs, the father the child needs? It felt like I would fail at everything.

'Here,' the boy said suddenly.

He'd been watching me closely, and now he reached into the pocket of his shorts and pulled something out.

A shell. Milky white and spiral in shape.

'It's pretty,' I said.

He gave a proud little sniff, like he was showing off a treasured prize.

'It's a lucky charm.'

'Oh yeah?'

'For you.'

There was a trace of reluctance in his expression, but then he held it out to me, straight and steady. Maybe he was trying to cheer me up. His gesture touched me. My chest grew warm.

'Thank you.'

I took the shell from him carefully, holding back the emotions welling up inside. It was still warm from his pocket. The moment it touched my hand, I heard the sound of waves. A powerful sense of déjà vu washed over me – waves crashing, the milky-white seashell, the boy's steady gaze. Was it a memory from the distant past? A glimpse of a faraway future? It felt like both. A *nostalgic future.*

I turned to him and confessed, 'When I get out of here . . . there's something I have to decide.'

'Decide what?'

'About the future.' I gave him a small smile and murmured, 'One more to go,' as if to rally myself. Then I took his warm hand and began to walk.

We rounded the corner and there it was again – the long white underground passage. The ↑ Exit 8 sign glowed overhead.

'To Exit 8 . . .'

'Let's go,' the boy replied.

'Dental Clinic . . . Escher Exhibit . . .'

As we checked the posters, I heard it – the distant sound of waves. Was it an anomaly? I strained my ears. The sound of sirens began to layer over the waves.

I froze. Pulling the boy close, I looked down the passageway.

The ground shook. A low rumble. One siren, then another, then more, until the whole passage echoed with the sound, like the roar of some monstrous beast. It was the same sound I'd heard on the TV that day, sitting in the dark room with my ex, just after the quake: sirens screaming mercilessly through a town swallowed by the tsunami.

'Shit . . .'

I grabbed the boy, trying to turn back. Grey water was already rushing in from the far end of the passage. The water rose in an instant, surging upwards into a towering wave that threatened to swallow the ceiling.

'Run!' I shouted, turning back.

'Hurry!' I yanked the boy's hand, but he stumbled and fell. I looked over my shoulder. He was lying face down on the floor. My breath caught. He raised his face, reaching out a hand towards me.

Behind him, the grey wave loomed like a monster swallowing up rubble. He looked up at me, a pleading look in his eyes. Was he asking me to save him? Or to save myself? I couldn't tell.

What do we do?

Her voice echoed in my ears. Would I look away again? Add one more sin to the pile?

No.

I spun round and sprinted towards the boy. Inhaling deeply, I reached out my hand – and in that moment, the tsunami swallowed us whole.

The foul, muddy water flooded into my lungs. I couldn't breathe. My ears, blocked by pressure, still caught the deafening clatter of debris smashing together. Inside the vortex of the wave, clothes, furniture, books, musical instruments, appliances, dishes – the clutter of human life spun past me.

There was no resisting it. The violence of the wave was too great.

All I could do was surrender. And as I gave in, a sense of peace began to wash over me. The yellow sign ↑ Exit 8 sign spun slowly before my eyes, growing more and more distant.

Was the boy safe? As my consciousness faded, I prayed. Please . . . let him live. And just as the darkness closed in, a single golden light pierced through.

3

6 The Sea

I raised a hand to shield my eyes from the dazzling sun. Golden rays streamed through the gaps between my fingers. Beside me, someone laughed.

'Oh no, I'm soaked.'

I turned to see her standing there – the woman I loved, smiling softly. The scent of the sea filled my nose, telling me exactly where we were. We stood side by side on a shallow beach, the water reflecting the sky like a mirror.

Out in the distance, a child played by the water's edge. A boy? A girl? I couldn't tell – the face was hidden by the glare of the sun behind them. The surface of the sea shimmered like scales catching the light.

'Daddy!' The child waved at me.

Daddy? Was he calling *me*? I turned to the woman at my side, confused.

'What are you going to do?' she asked, grinning playfully. 'You're being called.'

I gave her a bewildered smile, and she leaned in to whisper. A warm sea breeze stirred her long hair, carrying a soft floral scent to me.

'So,' she asked, 'are you going . . . or not?'

Apparently, I was a father in this world.

Still dazed, I looked at her, and then the child came running towards us, holding something in both hands.

'Mummy, look!'

In that small hand, wet from seawater and dusted with sand, was a milky-white seashell. It was a perfect spiral.

'How pretty!'

She smiled as she looked at the seashell. 'How about we make it your lucky charm?' she suggested.

Our son lit up, clearly loving the idea. He held out the shell to show me.

'Daddy, look! My lucky charm!

I crouched down and looked into his face – they were the same eyes that had stared at me so intently in the underground passage.

'Huh . . .'

I couldn't speak. Was this really my son?

Was this the future I saw after being swallowed by the waves in that tunnel? Or was it something else entirely?

A story I'd once read came back to me – Zhuangzi's *Butterfly Dream*.

Long ago, in that old school by the sea, I had read about a man who dreamed he was a butterfly. He fluttered through the air, free and light, with no idea he was human. But when he woke up, he didn't know – had he dreamed he was a butterfly, or was the butterfly dreaming it was him?

'What do we do?' she had asked me. And now, here was the future I had chosen, standing right in front of me.

I was supposed to be seeing what lay ahead, but it felt more like a memory from long ago. A warm, distant memory. Tears welled up in my eyes.

'Daddy?' the boy said, tilting his head. 'You okay?'

He gently rubbed my back with his little hand. That warmth undid me. I couldn't hold the tears in anymore.

I had met this child before.

'I'm going ahead!' he called, already running back to the edge of the waves, leaving me behind in my tears.

'Hey, you okay?' she asked softly, taking my arm as I stood up and wiped my face with my sleeve.

'Am I . . . a good father?'

'What's wrong?'

'Sometimes I just feel lost.'

She responded with a wry smile, 'You've always been bad with directions.'

She was right. In the past, in the future – and even now – I was still lost.

Seeing me stay quiet, she went on, 'No one knows for sure which path is the right one.'

The boy's voice drifted over, mingling with the sound of the surf. It was the same soft voice I had heard in that underground passage.

'Don't worry,' she said, her gaze full of tenderness as she looked towards our son. 'You'll protect that boy.'

Then, with a faint smile, 'And someday, that boy will protect you.'

It sounded like a prophecy about the past. I would protect him, and he would protect me.

'I'm going,' I murmured, her words giving me courage.

'Go on, then,' she said, giving my back a firm pat to send me off.

I kicked off my shoes and ran. The hard-packed sand pressed against the soles of my feet. I sprinted towards the boy splashing at the edge of the sea. When I stepped into the water, it was colder than I expected, but the chill felt good.

'Dad! Be careful!'

We stood side by side at the shoreline, dodging the waves as they rolled in, then chasing them as they drew back.

'Here it comes! Here it comes!' he shouted.

A big wave surged towards us, the spray leaping high. Salt water touched my lips. The swell kept rising, reaching for his little legs.

'Look out!'

In a heartbeat, I slipped my hands under his arms, dug my toes deep into the sand and lifted him high. His small feet left the water just as the foaming white wave crashed beneath us. The boy's body, held aloft in my arms, seemed to melt into the golden ring of sunlight.

7 Exit 8

Everything is mouse-grey.

I'm being swept away in muddy water. I can't breathe. It feels like I've been thrown into a washing machine, my arms and legs are all twisted up, like they're about to fall off. I'm sorry, Mummy. I got lost on purpose, so now I'm getting punished. I'm sorry, Mummy. I'm sorry, I'm sorry. Please help me.

I can't breathe, and the grey in front of my eyes is slowly turning cream-coloured. Maybe I should just go to sleep. If I go to sleep, all the scary and sad things will go away.

All of a sudden, someone lifts me up. Everything turns bright yellow. I rub my muddy eyes and see it: the ↑ Exit 8 sign. Even with the giant wave all around us, the sign was shining yellow.

'Hold on!' a voice shouts behind me. It's the young man. He's holding me tight and I grab the sign as hard as I can. My hands slip, and I almost fall, but I dig my nails

in and don't let go. He's hanging on to the sign too, right next to me.

Bicycles, traffic lights, microwave ovens, even pianos, float past us, smashing into the sign and making it shake. The man keeps holding me tight while still clinging on. He coughs hard, like his chest hurts from drinking so much water.

'It's gonna be okay,' he says, looking right at me.

'It's gonna be okay,' I say back, trying to believe it.

'We'll meet again,' he says, wiping my face with his hands.

I want to cry. Is this goodbye? If I say anything, I'm scared it will make it real. So I don't say a word.

Then – bang! – a huge noise, and the signboard shakes hard.

A big car, carried by the waves, crashes into us. The young man's hand slips off the sign.

'Hold on!'

I reach for him, but he just says, 'I'm okay,' and doesn't take my hand. The car pushes him away, and the water sweeps him off.

'Don't go!' I shout.

'Where are you?' I call again and again, but I can't see him anywhere. He's already far away, carried off by the water.

What should I do? Somebody help me. I'm scared. I'm cold. I'm so sleepy. I cling to the signboard, but my eyes keep getting heavier. Sleepy . . . so sleepy . . . The yellow sign in front of me slowly fades to a soft cream colour. Sleepy . . . sleepy . . . sleepy . . .

When I wake up, I'm lying on top of a broken piano. It's caked with mud, and its keys are scattered everywhere. It looks so sad. The wet floor is covered with shards of glass and splinters of wood. I push myself up with my hands. My mouth feels gritty, full of sand. My clothes are stuck to my skin. It feels awful. Is this the same path as before? Most of the lights are out, but one is flickering on and off. A bicycle with no tyre. A poster peeling from the wall. The photo booth with its mirror cracked. A coin locker hanging open without a door. Mud-covered books. All of them flash in the flickering light.

I feel warmth above my head so I look up at the ceiling. The yellow ↑ Exit 8 sign is glowing. Everything else is broken and muddy, but the sign shines so bright, like a god. Where's the young man? I turn back, picking my way through the rubble. It's hard to walk.

'Hello? Where are you?'

I peer into a boat washed in by the flood. I check inside a broken house. But he's nowhere to be found.

I give up and turn the corner. There it is – the straight white passage. White like someone painted it with thick paint. The same passage as always. I walk forwards, and then I see a yellow sign.

'Exit 8 . . .' I read out loud.

I finally made it to Exit 8. If the young man were here, we could've been happy together. I sit down under the Exit 8 sign and wait. But no matter how long I sit, he doesn't come. Maybe he already left. I stand up. I look back again and again as I turn the corner.

It's still the same long white passage, with the yellow ↑ Exit 8 sign.

'To Exit 8 . . .' I say again.

I start walking.

'Dentist . . . Escher . . . Judicial . . . Beauty . . .' I check for anomalies, just as the man used to. My wet shoes make a squishy sound as I walk. It's funny.

'Part-time . . . Manners . . . Security Cameras . . .'

Footsteps. The big man starts walking towards me.

'Big man . . .'

Like always, he walks straight ahead, not looking at me.

'Goodbye, Mister!' I say, waving at him. He keeps walking and then turns the corner. He didn't look sad. He's always walking, but maybe he's happy. I'm glad I got to say goodbye to him.

'Fire Hydrant . . . door . . . door . . . vent . . . door . . . vent . . .'

No anomalies. I turn the corner.

'Lockers . . . blankets . . . cups . . . photo booth . . . No anomalies.'

I take a few steps back and look down the path I just came from. The same straight white passage. The young man isn't coming.

'We'll meet again,' I say, just as he had said to me.

He'll be fine. I gave him the seashell I found at the beach when I went there with Mummy. It's a lucky charm, so he'll be okay.

I take a deep breath and turn the corner.

There's a staircase. 'Exit 8.'

I look up. Sunlight is pouring in from the exit. Voices. Lots of people talking. The sounds of cars and bikes. Birdsong. Music. I start climbing the stairs. My wet shoes go squish squish squish. It's so funny. I laugh. Squish. Squish. Squish. When I get home, I'll eat pizza with Mummy. Squish squish squish.

8 ANOTHER EXIT 8

'Last one,' I whispered when I saw the sign for Exit 8.

How many hours had passed since the tsunami had swallowed me?

Dragged under by the waves, I'd blacked out. When I came to, I was lying once again in the white passageway. The water and rubble were gone, but my clothes clung to me, heavy with seawater, and my mouth was gritty with sand. Those traces told me the tsunami had been real.

I rushed to look for the boy, but he was nowhere in sight.

That wave ... no doubt it was another anomaly. I'd turned back, only to find myself staring at the sign for Exit 0.

Reset to the very beginning. Despair washed over me. But when I felt the seashell charm still in my pocket, my resolve returned. It hadn't been a dream. The boy, my meeting with him, the future that lay ahead – none of it.

Saving the boy from the tsunami in this underground passage. The child she carried being born. Living as a father in the days to come. I no longer knew the order of things.

Did they belong to different parallel worlds? But I was sure they were connected. The life I longed for could only be reached through choices – hard, painful choices – made in the struggle between moving forwards and turning back.

Separated from the boy, I started over alone from Exit 0. Again and again, mistakes sent me back to the beginning, yet at last I had made it here, to the sign for Exit 8.

How long had it taken? Hours? Days? Maybe even weeks. Time itself had slipped away. But now, finally, the end was near.

I turned the corner – and there it was. The same endless white passage. And above me, glowing against the ceiling: the ↑ Exit 8 sign.

'Dental Clinic . . . Escher Exhibit . . . Judicial Services . . . Beauty Clinic . . .'

I scanned the signs more carefully than usual, searching for any trace of an anomaly. Turning the corner, I saw the salaryman walking towards me. I kept him in sight while my eyes flicked over the posters for part-time jobs and subway manners.

Then I heard it – footsteps stopping just behind me.

I turned back, hesitant. The salaryman was staring straight at me, his smile stretched tight, as if a rubber mask had been plastered onto his face – a familiar anomaly.

When I met the boy, I'd asked him, 'Are you alone? Or is there someone with you?' He'd pointed to this man. And I'd said, 'He's barely human.'

But maybe I was wrong. Maybe this man, too, had once struggled to escape, just like me. Maybe he'd been forced to face his sins and wander this passage in torment. Perhaps the boy had seen him when he was still human. If so, then he and I weren't so different. It could just as easily be me trapped down here, walking endlessly like some programmed robot.

'This is . . . an anomaly, isn't it?' I asked softly.

But the man only stared back, that frozen grin still fixed in place. His black pupils seemed out of focus, impossible to read. I peered into them, deeper and deeper. And there, far within, I saw a faint light. Two birds flying through it. Perhaps that was the last thing he saw as a human, and he had been walking ever since, forever dreaming of a bright, beautiful world outside.

As I retraced my steps, a question gnawed at me: which was happier? To keep walking, lost in a dream of happiness? Or to stumble through reality, never knowing what happiness was?

If I could find Exit 8, I wanted to break free of this lazy loop of reality.

I had to get out. To do that, I had to choose. Move forwards or turn back. Just before the corner, I glanced behind me.

Under the glowing yellow Exit 8 sign, the salaryman stood frozen, that wide grin still fixed on his face.

'Goodbye.'

Tears welled in my eyes. How many times had I passed him here? Never again would I cross paths with the same person so many times. In this endless white passage, I realised only now that his presence had been a kind of anchor for me.

Then I turned the corner. A staircase appeared before me.

But instead of joy, confusion struck first. The stairs did not climb upwards – they led deeper underground. Was this another anomaly? Or the true exit? I hesitated, pacing, peering down into the dim stairwell.

'What should I do . . .?'

Unable to decide, I gazed down at the seashell clutched in my hand. Suddenly, I heard the sound of waves. She was there beside me, smiling. The boy's face. The future I knew had to exist. That future pushed me forwards.

I set my foot on the first step and began to descend.

Carefully, I felt out each step as I moved deeper down the shadowed stairwell. I turned at a landing and kept going. Another landing, another turn. With every descent, faint sounds began to rise: the chime of ticket gates, the rumble of trains below. Another turn – and two young men in suits came climbing up towards me. I froze, startled. It had been so long since I'd seen another human being. Then a high-school boy came up, phone pressed to his ear, speaking into it as he passed.

Heat enveloped me, the thick, suffocating air of the subway station. Men, women, men, men, women . . . One after another, commuters brushed past, ascending the stairs. And there, ahead, I finally saw the station ticket gates. Drawn to the vending machine at their side, I stumbled forwards. With trembling hands I tapped my phone, grabbed a bottle, twisted the cap open and drank it down in one gulp. How long had it been – hours, days – since I'd last tasted water? As the liquid filled me, my vision seemed to clear. The haze lifted, and the world came into focus. I glanced back at the stairs. Streams of passengers poured upwards from the gates, climbing as though pulled by an unseen force. Were they, too, about to be swallowed into that endless loop of passageways? What kind of anomalies would they face there? What sins would they be forced to confront? Would they ever find Exit 8?

Or was that labyrinth meant only for me?

I pulled my earphones from my pocket, slipped them into my ears and dialled her number. Passing through the ticket gates, I started down the long stairway to the platform. Three rings. Four rings. Five rings. Still no answer. The platform slowly came into view. Six rings. Seven. And then, with the strains of *Boléro*, the train slid into the station. I ended the call and stepped aboard.

I wove my way through the crowd until I reached the opposite door, gripping the handrail. Again, *Boléro* echoed in my ears as the train pulled away. When the carriage entered the tunnel, I opened my messages.

What do we do?

Her text glowed on the screen. I stared at it, unable to reply. Then I heard a wail – it sounded like a newborn. I took out my earphones and shifted my gaze towards the sound. A woman was sitting in the priority seats, holding a crying baby in her arms. The subway carriage was packed. Commuters clung to straps and handrails, their eyes glued to their screens as if they couldn't hear the baby's cries.

'Shut that thing up!'

My shoulders jumped. I timidly turned my head to see who had shouted. A man in a suit stood across from the mother and baby. He ran a hand through his unkempt hair and trembled in his rumpled suit, his voice growing more heated.

'Everyone's sick of it! You're the mother – make it stop!'

My eyes flew wide. Was this a dream? Or an anomaly that had bled into reality? It wasn't the feeling of déjà vu but some kind of loop that I didn't have the words to explain. Cold drained from my chest down into my limbs. I turned back towards the window. I caught a glimpse of myself: white earphones dangling from my hand, pale skin, cracked lips and dark circles beneath bloodshot eyes.

No doubt remained. I hadn't escaped.

The baby's cries rose, sharper, louder. The man kept shouting. The mother cradled her child tighter. And all around us, the passengers stared into their screens, blank and unmoving. In the window, their faces floated in the blackness, eyes hollow, avoiding what they did not want to see. Eyes stained with sin, gazing straight back at me. Was this a present without an exit? Or the entrance to some future? The roar of the train pounded in my ears like *Boléro* – repeating, repeating, yet climbing, rising higher.

'Don't overlook the anomalies,' I whispered, staring at the reflection I had tried so long to ignore. The cough burned in my throat, but I swallowed it down, drawing a deep breath instead.

'Get out through Exit 8.'

I shoved through the crowd towards the shouting man.

EXIT

出口
Exit